Acting Edition

Superhero

Book by
John Logan

Music & Lyrics by
Tom Kitt

concord
theatricals

FOR PRODUCTION INQUIRIES

UNITED STATES AND CANADA
info@concordtheatricals.com
1-866-979-0447

UNITED KINGDOM AND EUROPE
licensing@concordtheatricals.co.uk
020-7054-7298

Each title is subject to availability from Concord Theatricals Corp., depending upon country of performance. Please be aware that *SUPERHERO* may not be licensed by Concord Theatricals Corp. in your territory. Professional and amateur producers should contact the nearest Concord Theatricals Corp. office or licensing partner to verify availability.

No one shall make any changes in this title(s) for the purpose of production. No part of this book may be reproduced, stored in a retrieval system, scanned, uploaded, or transmitted in any form, by any means, now known or yet to be invented, including mechanical, electronic, digital, photocopying, recording, videotaping, or otherwise, without the prior written permission of the publisher. No one shall share this title(s), or any part of this title(s), through any social media or file hosting websites.

For all inquiries regarding motion picture, television, online/digital and other media rights, please contact Concord Theatricals Corp.

THIRD-PARTY MATERIALS USE NOTE

Licensees are solely responsible for obtaining formal written permission from copyright owners to use copyrighted third-party materials (e.g., incidental music not provided in connection with a performance license, artworks, logos) in the performance of this play and are strongly cautioned to do so. If no such permission is obtained by the licensee, then the licensee must use only original materials and materials that the licensee owns and controls. Licensees are solely responsible and liable for clearances of all third-party copyrighted materials, and shall indemnify the copyright owners of the play(s) and their licensing agent, Concord Theatricals Corp., against any costs, expenses, losses and liabilities arising from the use of such copyrighted third-party materials by licensees. For music, please contact the appropriate music licensing authority in your territory for the rights to any incidental music not provided in connection with a performance license.

IMPORTANT BILLING AND CREDIT REQUIREMENTS

If you have obtained performance rights to this title, please refer to your licensing agreement for important billing and credit requirements.

SUPERHERO received a staged reading at the Eugene O'Neill Theater Center's National Music Theater Conference in July 2017 in Waterford, Connecticut. It was developed at Second Stage Theater in 2015, and it received its world premiere at Second Stage (Carole Rothman, President & Artistic Director; Casey Reitz, Executive Director; Christopher Burney, Artistic Producer) in New York, New York on January 31, 2019. The performance was directed by Jason Moore, with musical staging by Lorin Latarro, set design by Beowulf Boritt, costumes by Sarah Laux, lights by Jen Schriever, sound by Brian Ronan, projections by Tal Yarden, illusions by Chris Fisher, orchestrations by Michael Starobin and Tom Kitt, music direction by Bryan Perri, and music coordination by Michael Aarons. The stage manager was Diane DiVita. The cast was as follows:

SIMON	Kyle McArthur
CHARLOTTE	Kate Baldwin
DEAN FULTON	Nathaniel Stampley
VIC	Thom Sesma
JIM	Bryce Pinkham
VEE	Salena Qureshi
RACHEL	Julia Abueva
DWAYNE	Jake Levy

CHARACTERS

In order of appearance:

SIMON

CHARLOTTE

DEAN FULTON

VIC

JIM

VEE

RACHEL

DWAYNE

Company members also perform **VOICES** when noted and available.

SETTING

A city.

Fire escape / roof, Charlotte and Simon's apartment, Dean's office, apartment building, high school cafeteria, laundry room, rooftop.

TIME

The present.

SONGS

ACT I

"The Adventures of the Amazing Sea-Mariner"...............Simon

"What's Happening to My Boy?"......................... Charlotte

"The Adventures of the Amazing Sea-Mariner (Reprise)".......Simon

"You Don't Know What I Know"............................... Jim

"The Man in 4B" ....Charlotte & Simon

"I'll Save the Girl"..Simon

"The Man in 4B (Reprise)"......................Charlotte & Simon

"Laundry For Two"..................................... Charlotte

"I'll Save the Girl (Reprise)".................................Simon

"The Man in 4B (Reprise 2)".....................Charlotte & Simon

"The Adventures of the Amazing Sea-Mariner (Reprise 2)" ......Simon

"How Do You Do This Again? /
You Don't Know What I Know (Reprise)"...... Jim, Charlotte & Simon

ACT II

"It's Not Like in the Movies" .... Jim

"The Man in 4B (Reprise 3)".....................Charlotte & Simon

"The Adventures of the Amazing Sea-Mariner (Reprise 3)" ......Simon

"If I Only Had One Day" .... Vee & Simon

"In Between".................................... Charlotte & Jim

"My Dad, the Superhero" ....Simon

"It Happens to You"...................................... Charlotte

"What Are the Words?"................................... Charlotte

"If I Only Had One Day (Reprise)"..........................Simon

"Superman is Dead".......................................Simon

"Superhero"... Charlotte

ACT I

Prelude
Fire Escape

(**SIMON** *is alone on the fire escape outside his apartment, drawing. This is his refuge from the world and the dissonance in his life.*)

(*He's about fifteen years old.*)

[MUSIC NO. 00 "PRELUDE"]

(*Music...a glorious fanfare. Brave superheroic themes with a soaring orchestral sweep.*)

(**SIMON** *draws happily, inspired.*)

[MUSIC NO. 01 "THE ADVENTURES OF THE AMAZING SEA-MARINER"]

SIMON.
UP ABOVE, THE SUN IS RISING.
BUT DOWN BELOW, THE WORLD IS BURNING.
DOWN BELOW THERE'S CHAOS AND CRUELTY, DISORDER AND FEAR.
BUT UP ABOVE, THERE IS PEACE.
UP ABOVE, THERE IS HOPE.
A WORLD OF TRANQUILITY
WHERE YOU'RE SAFE WITH THE ONES YOU HOLD DEAR.
AND YOU WISH IT COULD STAY
EXACTLY THIS WAY...
BUT YOU KNOW THAT THREATS ARE LURKING EV'RYWHERE.

SO LOOK UP HIGH –
WAY UP IN THE SKY –
HE IS THERE!

"The Adventures of the Amazing Sea-Mariner"...Issue Number One by Simon Branson.

> *(Music... He begins to draw feverishly.)*

> *(Images appear to illustrate his story as he creates it.)*

THE SEA-MARINER, RULER OF OCEANS.
PROTECTOR AND GUARDIAN OVER HIS DOMAIN.
THE SEA-MARINER, SEEKER OF JUSTICE
HE CAN HEAL THE WORLD'S SUFF'RING AND PAIN.

DEFENDER OF THE SMALL AND THE MEEK
A SAVIOR TO ALL THOSE IN NEED.
IN THESE DARK TIMES WHERE EACH DAY LOOKS BLEAK
HOW LUCKY WE ARE...
HOW LUCKY, INDEED.

But like all mighty heroes, he has a mighty foe, a villain who takes joy in polluting the oceans and threatening the Sea-Mariner's realm...

CRUSH, HIS EPIC ARCH-NEMESIS
CRUSH, OF THE UNHOLY GENESIS
WHOSE PARTNERS IN CRIME ARE THE SLUDGE AND THE SLIME
THAT HE LEAKS INTO RIVERS AND SEAS...
THERE IS NO CURE FOR THIS DISEASE.

AND HE HUNGERS FOR THE GIRL
WHO LIVES AT THE TOP OF THE WORLD
SHE'S THE ONLY THING HE NEEDS
THE ONLY THING THAT'S PURE
HE KNOWS THAT HE MUST HAVE HER
HE'S NEVER FELT SO SURE
SO HE CLIMBS WAY UP AND TAKES HER

AND BRINGS HER TO HIS CAVE...

(Revises.) Dungeon?

(Revises.) Duplex?

LAIR –

SHE HASN'T A PRAYER...

CRUSH CREEPS UP BEHIND HER

WHISPERS, "I'M MUCH KINDER THAN YOU GIVE ME
  CREDIT FOR."

HE SHUTS THE DOOR

BEGINS TO PANT...

(Whispered panting noise.) HUH, HUH, HUH

HE OPENS HIS MOUTH...

HE OPENS HIS MOUTH...

AND BIT BY BIT SHE KNOWS THIS IS IT!

BUT JUST AS SHE'S ABOUT TO FADE AWAY...

THE SEA-MARINER COMES TO SAVE THE DAY!

AND SO, THERE THE BATTLE BEGINS

THE FIGHT FOR THE RIGHT TO LIVE ON.

FOR THE SEA-MARINER KNOWS IF CRUSH WINS

WE WILL ALL SOON BE GONE.

IT WILL ALL BE GONE...

SO, THE SEA-MARINER FLIES INTO ACTION

HE'S NEVER FELT SO STRONG OR MOVED SO FAST.

AND CRUSH COMES RUSHING AT HIM,

BUT THE SEA-MARINER KILLS HIM –

AT LAST! –

	VOICES.
AND ORDER'S RESTORED	OOH –
THE WORLD IS SAFE	OOH –
AND THE GIRL IS SO	OOH –
GRATEFUL...	
THE WEDDING'S IN APRIL...	
EV'RYTHING'S OKAY...	
BUT WAIT –	

VOICES.
AHH –

SIMON.
WAIT –

VOICES.
AHH –

SIMON.
SOMETHING'S MOVING

VOICES.
AHH –

SIMON.
CRUSH IS MOVING

VOICES.
AHH –

> (**SIMON**'s *drawing becomes more desperate
> as he tries to control his story, the brutal
> escalation of the song invading his mind –)*

HE'S NOT DEAD...
TURN AROUND
PLEASE!
HE'S COMING
HE'S COMING
HE'S COMING

> (*At the agonizing crescendo of the song, he
> screams:)*

MOVE! LOOK OUT!

> (*Then:)*

> (*A door to the roof opens.)*

> (**CHARLOTTE** *stands, framed in the doorway.)*

CHARLOTTE. Simon, are you all right? I thought I heard
you call out...

*(**SIMON** instantly tucks away the comic book he's been drawing as **CHARLOTTE** enters.)*

(She's carrying some papers she's been grading. She's an Associate Professor of Literature at a midsized college. She's a bit disheveled and casually dressed, not for work.)

SIMON. No. It's nothing.

CHARLOTTE. *(Re: his drawing.)* Can I see?

SIMON. You wouldn't understand it.

CHARLOTTE. I do have an advanced degree you know.

SIMON. It's private.

CHARLOTTE. Okay. Come on, you're going to be late.

(They go into the apartment.)

(And we are at...)

Scene One
Charlotte and Simon's Apartment

(The apartment is somewhat disorganized. There are books everywhere. The detritus of Charlotte's academic life: her own research, her student's papers, mountains of Romantic poetry books, etc.)

(Also, a messy stack of Simon's beloved comic books.)

(**SIMON** *starts packing up his things for school.*)

SIMON. *(Re: her papers.)* How's John Clare coming?

CHARLOTTE. Mad as ever.

SIMON. Pick a sane poet to write about next time... Aren't you getting dressed?

CHARLOTTE. I'm letting a grad student cover my classes today.

SIMON. Again.

CHARLOTTE. What?

SIMON. Nothing.

CHARLOTTE. Thought I would organize the books or something. Tidy up, you know. Half my clothes are still in boxes.

SIMON. Only I thought you had faculty review coming up?

CHARLOTTE. Don't remind me. Ugh, can't think about that today. And I really have to work on the book.

SIMON. *(Re: his stack of comic books.)* Don't "tidy up" up my comics, okay? There's an *order* to them.

CHARLOTTE. *(Dry.)* Yeah. I can see that.

> (**SIMON** *starts to go, but* **CHARLOTTE**'*s got something on her mind. She knows this is dangerous territory...*)

Hey, Mr. Fletcher called again... The stonemason's been waiting.

SIMON. Uh-huh.

CHARLOTTE. Would be great if you had something you wanted to say about your dad.

SIMON. Not really.

CHARLOTTE. I could use your help, you're so creative...

> (*No response.*)

...Come on. Can we talk about all this?

SIMON. You have to go, Mom. You're going to be late again.

CHARLOTTE. *Hold on.* Can you just listen to me?

> (**SIMON** *looks at her, at once defiant and vulnerable.*)

If we work on this together...picking the words... I think it will help.

SIMON. Help *you* you mean.

CHARLOTTE. Both of us.

SIMON. Can we talk about this later?

CHARLOTTE. *Honey, we have to talk about it.*

SIMON. (*With sudden emotion.*) Honestly, I don't think we do. Like at this moment.

CHARLOTTE. But if we don't talk about it then –

SIMON. (*Tears coming.*) I have to go to school, okay?! And I have to smile at everyone and "make new friends" and then you want me to talk about the accident every two minutes – and that's supposed to help me?! You know what? *It doesn't.*

(He goes quickly.)

[MUSIC NO. 02 "WHAT'S HAPPENING TO MY BOY?"]

(She stands there for a moment. She's failed to make a connection. Again.)

CHARLOTTE.
TEARS IN HIS EYES.
ANGER AND FEAR.
HOW DID WE BOTH END UP HERE?
LIVING EACH DAY LIKE WE'RE BARELY THERE.
AND WHERE DO THE ANSWERS LIE?
THERE HAS TO BE MORE THAN JUST GETTING BY.

WHAT'S HAPP'NING TO MY BOY?
WHAT'S HAPPENED TO HIS SMILE?
WE HAVEN'T HAD AN EASY TIME IN QUITE A WHILE.

WHAT'S HAPP'NING TO MY BOY?
SO YOUNG AND YET HE'S SEEN SO MUCH.
RUNNING FROM HIS MOTHER'S LOVE,
A STRANGER TO HER TOUCH

BUT I HAVE TO FIND MY WAY
I HAVE TO FIND MY WAY
I HAVE TO FIND MY WAY
I HAVE TO FIND MY WAY
THROUGH THIS NEVER-ENDING NIGHT
SO HOLD ON TIGHT

VOICES.
HOLD ON –
TIGHT –

CHARLOTTE.
WHAT'S HAPP'NING TO MY BOY?
WHERE DOES HE SOMETIMES GO?
A LIFE IT SEEMS OF BROKEN DREAMS, DON'T I KNOW.

IS THERE A BOOK TO READ
THAT TELLS ME HOW I PERSEVERE?
SOME WISDOM THAT WILL HELP ME FACE ANOTHER
    CRUSHING YEAR

CHARLOTTE.	VOICES.
BUT I HAVE TO FIND MY WAY	HOLD
I HAVE TO FIND MY WAY	ON
I HAVE TO FIND MY WAY	HOLD
I HAVE TO FIND MY WAY	ON
FIND A WAY FOR US TO	HOLD
HEAL...	ON

'CAUSE I'M REELING
WHILE YOU'RE RUNNING AWAY
I TRY TO TALK TO YOU
BUT YOU'VE GOT NOTHING TO SAY.
BUT DO WE GIVE UP OR FIGHT?
DO WE GO ON DESPITE WOND'RING
HOW WE'LL GET THROUGH THE DAY...

    (She finds one of Simon's drawings. Something
    about it unsettles her.)

WHERE ARE YOU BOY?
WHAT ARE YOU HIDING?
WHEN WILL YOU TRUST ME WITH ALL THAT YOU'VE
    SEEN?
AND WHEN WILL WE BE A FAM'LY ONCE AGAIN?
WHEN?

CHARLOTTE.	VOICES #1.	VOICES #2, #3 & #4.
		(Variously.)
BUT I HAVE TO FIND MY WAY,	I HAVE TO FIND MY WAY,	HOLD
I HAVE TO FIND MY WAY,	I HAVE TO FIND MY WAY,	
	AND HOLD ON,	ON (AND HOLD ON)

CHARLOTTE.	VOICES #1.	VOICES #2, #3 & #4.
I HAVE TO FIND MY WAY,	I HAVE TO FIND MY WAY,	HOLD
I HAVE TO FIND MY WAY,	I HAVE TO FIND MY WAY,	
	AND HOLD ON	ON (AND HOLD ON)

CHARLOTTE & VOICES #4.	VOICES #1, #2 & #3.
	(Variously.)
I HAVE TO FIND MY WAY,	HOLD
I HAVE TO FIND MY WAY,	ON (AND HOLD ON)
I HAVE TO FIND MY WAY,	HOLD
I HAVE TO FIND MY WAY,	ON.

CHARLOTTE.	VOICES.
FIND MY WAY BACK TO YOU,	HOLD ON.
THAT'S WHAT I'LL DO	
THAT'S WHAT I'LL DO.	

Scene Two
The Dean's Office of the University
Where Charlotte Teaches

(**CHARLOTTE** *enters* **DEAN FULTON***'s office.*
He's understanding, but he's got a job to do.
There's a sternness to him.)

DEAN FULTON. Charlotte?

CHARLOTTE. Justin? ...You wanted to see me.

DEAN FULTON. Come in. Sit down... I happened to see your lesson plan for Poetry 301. It's two years old.

CHARLOTTE. I've been meaning to update it. But, I mean, it's not like nineteenth-century Romantic Poetry has changed much in the last two years.

(*The joke falls flat.*)

(**CHARLOTTE** *knows exactly why she's here.*)

DEAN FULTON. Charlotte, you've been on the tenure track for six years now. The senior faculty has to make some decisions.

CHARLOTTE. You mean I need to publish.

DEAN FULTON. I mean more than that. You miss office hours, you cancel classes, you're late with grades. And, yes, you haven't published anything in two years. I was really looking forward to your book on John Clare, you were so close.

CHARLOTTE. The final research is complicated. It's obscure journals and British broadsides and periodicals I still have to track down. I can't publish until I've sourced the citations and –

DEAN FULTON. Charlotte. Be honest with me.

CHARLOTTE. ...My son needs me.

DEAN FULTON. Of course... But our students pay for a full-time education and they need full-time teachers. Your grad students are lost without you there.

CHARLOTTE. I know.

DEAN FULTON. We'll do anything we can to help, but I need you here. And I need you teaching. And yes, I need you publishing. The faculty review board meets next month, so please try... How's Simon, is he okay?

CHARLOTTE. Yeah. We moved a couple months ago, so he's starting at a new school. It's tough. But he's all right...

(She stops. The emotion comes unbidden.)

No, he's not. How could he be? ...He saw his father die. That's in his head, all the time. He's anything but all right... But I'll handle it. And I'll get working on the book.

DEAN FULTON. Thanks. And my door is always open.

CHARLOTTE. I appreciate it.

(She goes.)

[MUSIC NO. 02A "THE APARTMENT BUILDING"]

(She's been shaken by the encounter. Even though she knew something like this was coming, the reality is sobering.)

(She exits.)

Scene Three
The Apartment Building

(A somewhat rundown apartment building.)

(VIC, the truculent landlord/super, is sitting on an old plastic lawn chair up on the stoop. He's a big sloppy man. He's currently flipping through an old comic book.)

(There's an old mailbox on the curb.)

(SIMON is on his usual perch on the fire escape, drawing.)

(SIMON generally stays clear of the surly landlord. But he's intrigued by the comic book VIC is flipping through... SIMON cranes to see.)

VIC. What you looking at?

SIMON. What? Nothing.

VIC. *(Re: the comic book.)* What, this?

SIMON. It looks old.

VIC. It is. Just like me. And its feet hurt too.

SIMON. Can I see?

VIC. No.

SIMON. Why not?

VIC. 'Cause you're a kid and all kids are covered with pixie sticks and snot.

SIMON. What's a pixie stick?

VIC. Why do I waste my breath?

SIMON. So what's the comic?

VIC. From before you were born. Galaxy Man. "Return of the Superhero."

SIMON. Where did he go?

VIC. Were you raised under a rock? The superhero always dies – then comes back. It's *drama*... Forget it. Don't touch my shit.

> *(He lumbers into the building.)*

> *(**SIMON** thinks about it, an idea forming...)*

SIMON. The Superhero Returns...

> ### [MUSIC NO. 03 "THE ADVENTURES OF THE AMAZING SEA-MARINER (REPRISE)"]

> *(He starts to draw in his pad...)*

The Adventures of the Amazing Sea-Mariner, Issue Number Two! ...We think the Sea-Mariner has returned forever to his secret undersea realm. But no! He hears a voice crying out. Someone needs him! So he raises his head and coils his mighty muscles...

SIMON.	VOICES.
AND RISING UP ONCE AGAIN!	OOH
THE SEA-MARINER SENSES DANGER'S NEAR...	
AND HE KNOWS	AHH
HE MUST MAKE HASTE	AHH
THERE ISN'T TIME TO	AHH

> ### [MUSIC NO. 04 "YOU DON'T KNOW WHAT I KNOW"]

WASTE...	AHH...

> *(**JIM** enters, dressed in a bus driver's uniform. He's upset, tense.)*

> *(Just as **VIC** emerges from the building to retrieve his comic book.)*

> (**SIMON** *stops drawing and watches them,*
> *intrigued. They don't notice him up on the*
> *fire escape.*)

VIC. Jeez. You look like you're carrying the weight of the world.

JIM. I just got fired.

VIC. Yeah, that'll do it.

JIM. Dispatcher said I missed too many shifts. Everyone misses a few damn shifts. You don't fire someone for it.

VIC. I guess sometimes you do... Hey, you gonna have a problem with the rent now?

JIM. You're all heart, Vic.

> (**VIC** *takes his comic book and goes into the*
> *building.*)

> (**JIM** *is alone for a moment.* **SIMON** *watches*
> *him.*)

"Carrying the weight of the world..."

> (*He seems to find this bitterly amusing. His*
> *anger builds.*)

JIM.	VOICES.
YOU DON'T KNOW WHAT I KNOW...	
	HELP ME, HELP ME...
YOU DON'T KNOW WHAT I KNOW...	HELP HELP HELP HELP HELP HELP
	HELP ME, HELP –
YOU DON'T KNOW WHAT I –	HELP ME, HELP
YOU DON'T KNOW WHAT I –	ME, HELP ME,

JIM.	VOICES.
YOU DON'T KNOW WHAT I KNOW.	HELP ME, HELP ME!

(At the crescendo of the song:)

*(**SIMON** watches from above as **JIM** raises a fist, and with one furiously impossible blow flattens the mailbox! Superhero-like strength.)*

(Wow!)

*(**JIM** stops, looks at the mailbox.)*

(He glances around to make sure no one is watching and then grabs the mailbox and pulls it up into shape again. Another act of superhero-like strength.)

*(Then **JIM** turns – and hurries offstage.)*

[MUSIC NO. 04A "THE MAILBOX"]

*(**SIMON** gapes. Stunned.)*

VOICES.
AHH...

Scene Four
Charlotte and Simon's Apartment

[MUSIC NO. 05 "THE MAN IN 4B"]

(CHARLOTTE is going through heavily-notated books of John Clare poetry, making notes. The troubled nineteenth-century poet is her area of academic specialty.)

(SIMON enters.)

SIMON.
YOU KNOW THE BUS DRIVER?

CHARLOTTE.
WHAT?

SIMON.
THE BUS DRIVER? THE MAN IN 4B.

CHARLOTTE.
OH, YES THE BUS DRIVER. HE RARELY TALKS TO ME.
WHAT ABOUT HIM?

SIMON.
I SEE HIM NOW AND THEN.

CHARLOTTE.
ARE WE SPEAKING AGAIN?

SIMON.
MOM, DO YOU KNOW THE GUY?

CHARLOTTE.
WHY?

(Silence, then:)

I DID ONCE RING HIS DOORBELL
YOU'RE RIGHT. HE LIVES IN 4B.
HIS MAIL ONCE CAME TO US, MISTAKENLY.

SIMON.
> DID YOU SEE HIS APARTMENT?

CHARLOTTE.
> SIMON, WHY THE QUESTIONS?

SIMON.
> JUST CURIOUS, THAT'S ALL.

CHARLOTTE.
> THAT'S ALL?

SIMON.
> THAT'S ALL.

CHARLOTTE.
> HE CAME TO THE DOOR, TOOK THE MAIL AND THANKED
>> ME
> AND ACTUALLY HE WAS KIND OF...

SIMON. *(Spoken in rhythm.)*
> WHAT? SHIFTY?

CHARLOTTE.
> MAYBE SHY. AN UNASSUMING GUY.

SIMON.
> I THINK HE HAS A SECRET

CHARLOTTE.
> YOU THINK EV'RYONE HAS A SECRET
> LIKE THE TIME THAT YOU THOUGHT THE BAGEL GUY
>> WAS REX LUTHOR

SIMON.
> *LEX* LUTHOR.

CHARLOTTE.
> *LEX* LUTHOR. SORRY.
> ANYWAY, HE'S CLEARLY ON HIS OWN
> SO LEAVE THE MAN ALONE.

> *(More silence. But* **CHARLOTTE** *doesn't want*

> *to let this chance to communicate with her*
> *son pass...)*

AND YET I WONDER...

SIMON. *(Spoken in rhythm.)*
WHAT?

CHARLOTTE.
THERE IS SOMETHING, ABOUT THE MAN IN 4B
HE DOES HAVE AN AIR OF MYSTERY

SIMON. *(Spoken in rhythm.)*
SEE?!

CHARLOTTE.
I'M NOT SAYING...

SIMON.
WE SHOULD INVESTIGATE

CHARLOTTE.
WE SHOULD LEAVE THE MAN IN PEACE

SIMON.
WE SHOULD CALL THE POLICE.

CHARLOTTE.
HE HARDLY SEEMS AS IF HE'S THE CRIMINAL TYPE
IN FACT, I THINK HE SEEMS QUITE...

SIMON. *(Spoken in rhythm.)*
WHAT?

CHARLOTTE. *(Spoken in rhythm.)*
NORMAL,
(Sung.) EVEN NICE. KIND TO BE PRECISE.

SIMON.
IT SOUNDS LIKE YOU LIKE HIM

CHARLOTTE.
I DON'T EVEN KNOW HIM

SIMON.
> YOU JUST SAID HE WAS NICE

CHARLOTTE.
> NO I SAID NORMAL.

SIMON.
> AND NICE.

CHARLOTTE.
> I DID?

SIMON.
> YOU DID.

CHARLOTTE.
> I DID. I SEE IT IN HIS EYES.

SIMON.
> IT'S JUST HIS DISGUISE.

CHARLOTTE.
> HOW IS WHATSHERNAME?

SIMON.
> MOM, YOU'RE CHANGING THE SUBJECT.

CHARLOTTE.
> SIMON, I'M DONE WITH THE MAN IN 4B.

SIMON.
> HER NAME IS VEE.

CHARLOTTE.
> VEE.

SIMON.
> VEE LOOKS RIGHT THROUGH ME.

CHARLOTTE.
> SO STAND IN FRONT OF HER.

SIMON.
> MOM, THAT WOULD BE THE END.

CHARLOTTE.
SHE COULD DO WORSE FOR A FRIEND, THAN YOU.

SIMON.
BUT I'M COMPLICATED.

CHARLOTTE.
THAT'S TRUE.
BUT MAYBE SHE IS TOO.

(**SIMON** *thinks about it.*)

(**CHARLOTTE** *takes this opportunity, this moment of harmony, to bring something up. She tries to be casual...*)

Hey, Simon... I want to talk about something. Something I found...

(*She produces the comic book page she found before.*)

SIMON. That's supposed to be private!

CHARLOTTE. I know. But I just don't know what this means. I was –

SIMON. Why were you going through my stuff in the first place?!

CHARLOTTE. You never used to draw things like this. It's so dark and –

SIMON. So you're my therapist now?

CHARLOTTE. Is this why you stopped showing me your work? Is it all like this?

SIMON. This is exactly why I don't show you anything! You don't understand it.

CHARLOTTE. I'm trying to help!

SIMON. You can help by leaving me alone.

CHARLOTTE. If this is about your dad then we should –

SIMON. Stop it!

CHARLOTTE. It's been two years, Simon, we need to talk about it.

SIMON. It's a stupid fucking comic book!

(He snatches it from her and rips it to shreds.)

There! Now there's nothing to talk about! AND STAY OUT OF MY ROOM!

(He storms off. Slam!)

[MUSIC NO. 06 "WHAT'S HAPPENING TO MY BOY (REPRISE)"]

(CHARLOTTE stands there, stunned at how quickly things can turn bad between them. Frustrated and upset.)

(And feeling like the worst mother in the world.)

CHARLOTTE.
I HAVE TO FIND MY WAY
I HAVE TO FIND MY WAY
HELP ME...
HELP ME...

Scene Five
High School Cafeteria

(SIMON sits alone, away from everyone else, as he always does.)

(At another table, VEE sits with her friend RACHEL. They are seniors. Simon is a sophomore. VEE's a smart, dynamic girl with strongly-held beliefs.)

(SIMON has a mighty crush on VEE. He watches...)

VEE. I mean think about it. Between global warming and overpopulation and using up our natural resources it's like we're going to graduate into a world that's dying. This scientist was saying in a hundred years the planet's going to be *uninhabitable* – so we better start looking for a new planet to live on.

RACHEL. I call the Wonder Woman planet.

VEE. So I got totally inspired about it and asked the school to give us the cafeteria for a night, so we could do something. One night to figure out how we save the world in the next hundred years. Like a science fair – with art projects and speeches and whatever else.

RACHEL. Oh, shit, ex-boyfriend alert...

(She means DWAYNE, who has just entered. He's Vee's ex. Handsome but a bit too aggressive, without really meaning to be.)

I know he's a dick, but damn he is fine.

(DWAYNE goes to VEE... SIMON watches closely.)

DWAYNE. Vee, come on, this isn't human...

VEE. Not now, Dwayne.

RACHEL. Leave her be.

DWAYNE. Not your business, Rachel… *(Back to* **VEE**.*)* You break up with me by text? Who does that?!

[MUSIC NO. 07 "I'LL SAVE THE GIRL"]

SIMON. *(To himself.)* Now, Simon…

DWAYNE. And you ignore my calls.

RACHEL. Come on, Vee, let's roll.

DWAYNE. You can't take two seconds to call me back?

SIMON. *(To himself.)* Now, Simon. You can do it. Stand up. Walk over there…

DWAYNE. I mean who do you think you are?

RACHEL. Oh, step back.

VEE. Get away from me, Dwayne.

DWAYNE. *Just sit down.*

SIMON.
DO I HAVE THE STRENGTH?
CAN I FIND THE WILL?
COULD I SPRING TO ACTION, INSTEAD OF STANDING STILL?
COULD I SAVE HER?
WHAT IF I COULD FLY
WITH POWER AND WITH SPEED?
WHAT IF I HAD THE BRAINS
AND THE KNOWLEDGE TO SUCCEED?
I COULD SAVE HER…
IT ISN'T FAIR, THE WEAK ARE ALWAYS PREYED UPON
AND MESSED WITH EV'RY DAY.
IT ISN'T RIGHT THAT THOSE WHO CAN'T DEFEND THEMSELVES
ARE THE ONES WHO ALWAYS PAY.
I COULD CHANGE THAT

I COULD CHANGE THAT...
I'LL SAVE THE GIRL!
RIGHT HERE AND NOW.
THE ONLY THING IS –
I DON'T KNOW HOW.
BUT THERE HAS TO BE A MOMENT
WHEN A NEW HERO GRABS HIS CHANCE TO SHINE.
COULD THIS BE MINE?
IT'S MINE!
I'LL SAVE THE GIRL.

DWAYNE. You can't treat people like that.

VEE. Drop it, Dwayne.

DWAYNE. When did you turn into such a bitch?

RACHEL. Don't call her that –

DWAYNE. You stay out of it –

VEE. This has got nothing to do with her –

(**SIMON** *actually stands to help –*)

(**DWAYNE** *spins on him –*)

DWAYNE. *(Spoken in rhythm.)*
WHAT ARE YOU LOOKING AT?!

(**SIMON** *instantly sits.*)

SIMON.
WHAT THE HECK AM I THINKING?
HE'LL PULVERIZE MY FACE
HE'LL STUFF ME IN A LOCKER
I'LL BE GONE WITHOUT A TRACE
THIS IS CRAZY
SO I WILL WALK AWAY
STAY SAFE AND LIVE TO TELL
OR MAYBE I COULD TAKE HIM...

DWAYNE. *(Seeing* **SIMON** *eyeing him again, yells. Spoken in rhythm.)*
WHAT?!

SIMON. *(Spoken in rhythm.)*
NOTHING!
(Sung.) THAT DIDN'T GO SO WELL.
THIS IS CRAZY
BUT I LOOK AT HER, HER EYES SO WIDE, HER FEAR SO RECOGNIZABLE, SO REAL
CAN I JUST WALK AWAY AND LET THE VICTIM SUFFER WOUNDS THAT NEVER HEAL?
I COULD CHANGE THAT
I COULD CHANGE THAT
I'LL SAVE THE GIRL!
FOR ONCE, THIS DAY
MY MANY POWERS
ON DISPLAY.
I'VE BEEN STUCK IN SUCH A RUT, WAITING FOR THE WORLD TO SEND A SIGN
COULD THIS BE MINE?
IT'S MINE!
I'LL SAVE THE GIRL
WHOA, I'M GETTING TOO UNWOUND
WHOA, IT'S BEST TO NEVER LEAVE THE GROUND
'CAUSE ONCE YOU TAKE A STAND YOU BLOW YOUR COVER
EV'RY DAY YOU'RE PLAYING HIDE AND SEEK.
AND EVEN IF MY GESTURE SOMEHOW MOVES HER
IT'S HARD TO DATE THE BOY WHO DOESN'T SPEAK.
AND YET, THERE'S THE GIRL.
THERE'S ALWAYS THE GIRL...
IT'S TIME TO MAKE A DIFF'RENCE
IT'S TIME TO LET THEM KNOW
TIME TO STAND FOR SOMETHING
TIME TO LET MY FEARS ALL GO
I CAN DO THIS!

SHE'S WAITING FOR A HERO, AND I'M THE ONE WHO'S
    ANSWERING THE CALL
BUT EVEN AS I THINK THIS, I'M STILL SITTING HERE
    DOING NOTHING AT ALL
I COULD CHANGE THAT
I COULD CHANGE THAT...

(But, across the room, **VEE** *has had enough.*
She stands – gets right in **DWAYNE***'s face:)*

VEE. Maybe this Neanderthal bullshit actually works on some girls but let me tell you, son, you gotta raise your game to the human being level to have the right to speak to me. So take your shaggy ass out of my face before I unleash a world of humiliation on you. NOW GET THE FUCK GONE!

*(***DWAYNE*** exits...* **VEE** *sits.)*

SIMON.
    WELL THERE IT IS
    FOR ALL TO SEE.
    WHEN YOU'RE IN DANGER –
    CALL ON VEE.
    SHE IS FEARLESS AND COURAGEOUS, THE KIND OF HERO
        I COULD NEVER BE
    I DIDN'T SAVE THE GIRL...
    BUT CAN THE GIRL SAVE ME?

(He looks at **VEE**, *more smitten than ever.)*

Scene Five
The Laundry Room

[MUSIC NO. 07A "TRANSITION TO LAUNDRY ROOM"]

(The building's rundown laundry room in the basement. Old coin-operated washers and dryers. Fluorescent lights.)

*(**CHARLOTTE** is making notes in an academic journal as she does the laundry.)*

*(**SIMON** rattles down the stairs to her. They're still uneasy after their fight earlier.)*

SIMON. You have to sign this.

CHARLOTTE. What is it?

SIMON. Field trip permission slip.

> *(He hands **CHARLOTTE** a permission slip. She signs it, taking her time. Wants to take advantage of this chance to talk to him. Any chance to make a connection...)*

CHARLOTTE. ...So, how was school?

SIMON. Fine.

CHARLOTTE. Did you "learn" anything?

SIMON. No.

CHARLOTTE. Did you talk to anyone?

SIMON. No.

CHARLOTTE. What about Vee? Did you see her?

SIMON. No. Can I have that?

> *(**CHARLOTTE** finishes signing and hands him the permission slip.)*

CHARLOTTE. I could use some help with the laundry.

SIMON. I have homework.

CHARLOTTE. Go on.

> (**SIMON** *immediately starts to go –*)
>
> (*But as he heads up the stairs he sees something – suddenly stops – spins back and returns to her eagerly.*)

SIMON. Act natural!

CHARLOTTE. What?

SIMON. Act like yourself – only better!

> (**JIM** *enters down the stairs with his laundry.*)
>
> (*He stops abruptly when he sees them.*)

JIM. Oh, excuse me.

CHARLOTTE. No problem, this one's free.

> (**JIM**'s *sort of trapped now, too awkward to leave. He starts doing his laundry.*)
>
> (**SIMON** *eagerly jumps at the chance to investigate.*)

SIMON. Hi, I'm Simon and this is my mom, and you are?

JIM. Jim.

SIMON. You're the bus driver.

JIM. What? Yes. Used to be.

SIMON. Used to be what?

JIM. A bus driver. Well, I still am. Lost my job, looking for another. Another bus driving job I mean. That's what I do.

SIMON. Is it?

JIM. What?

CHARLOTTE. Simon...

SIMON. That must be interesting. Driving a bus. You must meet lots of people. What kind of people do you meet?

JIM. Um...people who ride the bus.

SIMON. I barely see you in the building. Do you work really long hours?

JIM. Oh, night shift sometimes.

SIMON. Like mailmen.

JIM. Like mailmen?

SIMON. They have to get up really early and take care of the mail – and the *mailboxes*. We had an "incident" with our mailbox.

JIM. An "incident"?

CHARLOTTE. *(To* SIMON.*)* What are you talking about?

JIM. Quarters. I have to get more quarters.

> *(He goes quickly, a little abruptly.)*

> **[MUSIC NO. 08 "THE MAN IN 4B (REPRISE)"]**

> *(Light tension, conversational but trying to be private.)*

SIMON.
> SEE, I TOLD YOU HE WAS WEIRD, DON'T YOU THINK HE'S WEIRD?

CHARLOTTE.
> SIMON!

SIMON.
> EVASIVE.

CHARLOTTE.
> HE IS NOT!

SIMON.

>HE'S GOT SECRETS!
>MOM, C'MON, YOU MUST ADMIT.

CHARLOTTE.

>WHAT?

SIMON.

>SOMETHING JUST DOESN'T FIT

CHARLOTTE.

>HE'S JUST DOING HIS LAUNDRY
>OH RIGHT, HOW SUSPICIOUS!
>AND GETTING MORE QUARTERS?
>MY GOD!
>SO YES, LET'S CALL THE POLICE.
>THEY'LL BOOK HIM FOR DOING CHORES.
>I DO LOVE THAT MIND OF YOURS.

SIMON.

>YOU THINK I'M CRAZY.

CHARLOTTE.

>I THINK YOU'RE SWEET.

SIMON. *(To himself.)*

>MOM! PLEASE! I NEED YOU. CAN'T YOU SEE?

CHARLOTTE. Oh, you do?

>SO WHAT IS IT YOU'RE ASKING OF ME?

SIMON. You've got to flirt with him.

CHARLOTTE. Come again.

SIMON. You've got to flirt with him. It's the only way!

CHARLOTTE. Only way for what?!

SIMON. Listen, this is how it works, you are so ignorant. The only people who get behind the superhero's mask are the *women they date*! You wanna find out who Batman is in real life? Ask Vicki Vale. Who's

Spiderman? Ask Mary Jane. You wanna know who Superman is? Who do you ask?

CHARLOTTE. I don't know, Alfred the butler?

SIMON. I am so depressed right now.

CHARLOTTE. I so hope I'm not following what you're saying...

SIMON. You have to flirt with him – then ask him to dinner!

CHARLOTTE. I will not!

SIMON. Totally! You have dinner and ask a lot of questions and before you know it –

> (**JIM** *enters again...* **CHARLOTTE** *and* **SIMON** *abruptly stop.*)

Hello, again.

JIM. Yeah. Hi.

SIMON. Well, I'll leave you two to get better acquainted. Bye!

> (*He quickly goes before* **CHARLOTTE** *can react.*)

CHARLOTTE. Sorry about that, he's at that curious age.

JIM. No problem.

> (*There's a sudden awkwardness between them.*)

CHARLOTTE. I have a big fish bowl filled with them.

JIM. What?

CHARLOTTE. Quarters.

JIM. You have fish?

CHARLOTTE. No, no, just quarters.

(Beat.)

I don't mind fish. Just don't have any.

JIM. Mm.

CHARLOTTE. Just the fish bowl.

> *(JIM pulls an old, wet Superman t-shirt from his machine. He holds it up in front of his chest for a second.)*

JIM. I think this is yours.

CHARLOTTE. Oh, sorry, that's Simon's. Glad you didn't find my panties.

> *(She's immediately horrified.)*

> *(Beat as they continue with their laundry.)*

JIM. *(Re: the washing machine.)* This one never works right.

CHARLOTTE. Sometimes if you lean on the machine it helps. It's unbalanced. Much like my life.

JIM. Thanks. I'll try that... I don't mind doing laundry mostly. Not much on ironing though.

CHARLOTTE. Me neither. Ironing was always my husband's job...

> *(JIM looks at her, she explains:)*

...My husband died two years ago.

JIM. I'm sorry. Must be hard for you guys.

CHARLOTTE. Yeah. We're sorting it out... *(Re: the Superman t-shirt.)* ...This t-shirt was my husband's, now Simon wears it. Still get a shock when I see it... But you get used to things.

JIM. Yeah. You get used to things and then they're your life.

CHARLOTTE. Mm. Guess so.

>   *(Beat.)*
>
>   *(She thinks about it. What the hell. Might as well...)*

Sooo...you from the city?

JIM. Um, not originally.

>   *(He offers nothing more.)*

CHARLOTTE. Me neither. Minnesota. My whole family's there. My brother comes to visit sometimes... I'm a teacher – well, assistant professor. English Literature. Romantic poetry mostly. You know. Byron and Shelley and you know. I'm working on a book about John Clare in fact. He's kind of obscure but –

JIM. I have to go. Bye.

>   *(He leaves quickly.)*
>
>   *(She's mystified at his abrupt exit.)*
>
>   *(Then she looks at the Superman t-shirt.)*

[MUSIC NO. 09 "LAUNDRY FOR TWO"]

CHARLOTTE.

>   I WISH THAT YOU WERE REAL...
>   I WISH THAT YOU WERE HERE...
>   TO SAVE ME FROM THIS LIFE –
>   BEFORE I DISAPPEAR...
>
>   HOW DID THIS COME TO BE?
>   SO MUCH HAS HAPPENED SO FAST
>   I KEEP TRYING TO RUN TOWARDS THE FUTURE
>   BUT I CAN'T SHAKE THE PAST.
>
>   SEE I THOUGHT THAT YOU'D BE HERE WITHOUT A DOUBT
>   HELPING ME TO FIGURE THIS ALL OUT

NOW IT'S LAUNDRY FOR TWO, WHERE THERE SHOULD BE THREE
LAUNDRY FOR TWO, JUST THE KID AND ME
DOESN'T COST AS MUCH AND THERE'S LESS TO FOLD
BUT THIS SINGLE MOTHER CRAP, IT SURE GETS OLD
TRY TO LOSE MYSELF IN THE BLUES AND WHITES
AND FORGET ALL THE COUNTLESS, LONELY NIGHTS
WHEN I'D SIT AND STEW, DOING LAUNDRY FOR TWO

THE PANTS THAT ARE TORN AT THE KNEE
THE SHIRT HE REFUSES TO WEAR
THE JERSEY HE BOUGHT AT THE GAME
WHEN YOU WEREN'T THERE
HE GREW FROM SMALL TO LARGE IN THE BLINK OF AN EYE.
AND IT MAKES ME FEEL LIKE MY LIFE HAS PASSED ME BY.

SO BACK TO LAUNDRY FOR TWO, ONE LOAD FOR EACH.
LAUNDRY FOR TWO, USE A BIT LESS BLEACH.
IT'S METHODICAL, YES. A COMFORT OF SORTS.
AND WHEN DID HE SWITCH TO BOXER SHORTS?
TRY TO CALM MYSELF AS THE CLOTHES START TO SPIN
AND NOT PANIC ABOUT THIS MESS WE'RE IN.
BUT IT'S HARD TO DO, WHEN IT'S LAUNDRY FOR TWO.

MY BOY NEEDS HIS FATHER.
AND I NEED MY HUSBAND.
IT ISN'T LIKE I'M ASKING FOR THE MOON
I'D SETTLE FOR A TEAR-FREE AFTERNOON
BUT I GET LAUNDRY FOR TWO.
AND DINNER FOR TWO.
AND EV'RYTHING, EV'RY DAY, ALWAYS FOR TWO!

(She's interrupted when **JIM** *comes down with a box of fabric sheets to leave with his dryer. She tries to cover her emotion.)*

CHARLOTTE. Oh, hey.

JIM. Hey... Fabric sheets. "Spring Rain." What can it hurt, right?

CHARLOTTE. Right.

JIM. You okay...?

CHARLOTTE. Mm.

> (**JIM** *looks at her holding the Superman t-shirt.*)

JIM. That shirt suits you.

> (*He goes.*)

CHARLOTTE.
> LAUNDRY FOR TWO, PLUS THE AWKWARD GUY.
> LAUNDRY FOR TWO, DID HE SEE ME CRY?
> HOW DID I GET SO FAR OFF TRACK?
> WILL I EVER BE ABLE TO FIND MY WAY BACK?
> I ONCE THOUGHT THIS WORLD WAS MADE JUST FOR ME.
> LIFE WAS ENDLESS POSSIBILITY.
> BUT THAT LIFE IS THROUGH...
> THERE'S NOTHING TO SAVE ME AND YOU
> FROM LAUNDRY FOR TWO.

Scene Six
The Building

(Late afternoon.)

(SIMON is again at his usual perch up on the fire escape. Drawing. He's wearing his dad's Superman t-shirt today.)

(VIC is at his usual perch as well, sitting on his old lawn chair on the stoop. He's flipping through another vintage comic book.)

(They seem to be ignoring each other, until...)

VIC. So you draw.

SIMON. What? Yeah, I draw.

VIC. You ever draw a comic book?

SIMON. That's all I draw.

    (VIC grunts.)

    (SIMON continues to draw. VIC continues to flip through the comic book.)

You got a lot of them.

VIC. Yeah. From when I was a snot-nose, right?

SIMON. You have a favorite? Like Spiderman or the Avengers or –?

VIC. No.

    (A silent beat.)

For me, it was the ads. The ads at the back.

SIMON. Like what?

VIC. You know, Sea Monkeys or X-Ray glasses or Be Strong Like Charles Atlas. Back in the day, this was. I liked the ads.

SIMON. Why?

VIC. Eh. I never believed in superheroes. But Sea Monkeys
you can believe in!

> *(He hands* SIMON *up the comic.)*

Here, live and learn kid… And I want it back. Without
snot all over it.

> *(He goes.)*

> (SIMON *opens the comic book and flips to the
> back. He reads:)*

SIMON. "Enter the Wonderful World of the Amazing Live
Sea Monkeys. Own a Bowlful of Happiness."

> *(He smiles. "A bowlful of happiness." What a
> lovely thought.)*

> *(Just then,* VEE *and* RACHEL *enter, passing
> the building on their way home from an
> afterschool event.)*

> (SIMON *instantly hides the comic book.)*

VEE. …And I think Lorenzo's making a diorama that shows
overpopulation – matching the projected birth rates.
So, I thought I'd make an actual *calendar* that counts
down the hundred years. How many endangered
species we're going to lose. How much deforestation.
How many days of drought. Chart the rise of coastal
waters…

RACHEL. That sounds great… And super fun! …How many
exhibits do we have so far?

VEE. Like, four.

RACHEL. How we gonna save the planet with four ideas?

> (SIMON *shocks himself when he suddenly
> blurts out:)*

SIMON. *Five!* – Five ideas! I'll make something.

> (**VEE** *and* **RACHEL** *stop.* **SIMON** *continues quickly, nervously, can't stop the words now...*)

I draw a lot so I could draw something like a – I have no idea – but something about healing the world. Like – like – a bowl full of happiness!

> (*He wilts. His romantic dreams dashed. But...*)

VEE. I would love it if you made something, Simon.

> (**SIMON**'*s shocked she even knows his name.*)

You're really talented in art class. And we need all the help we can get. Maybe we could get together tomorrow and talk about what you want to do?

SIMON. Get together! Okay. Wow. Yes.

VEE. Maybe after school?

SIMON. Well, I'll have to check my schedule... Ah, it's clear.

> (*He laughs awkwardly.* **VEE** *smiles, charmed.*)

VEE. Great. I have tutoring right after school, but I could meet you here around six. Is that okay?

SIMON. You bet!

VEE. See you then. Bye.

> **[MUSIC NO. 10 "I'LL SAVE THE GIRL (REPRISE)"]**

SIMON. Okay. Great. Vee. Thanks. Vee... Bye.

> (**VEE** *and* **RACHEL** *go.*)

> (**SIMON** *is utterly stunned at what he has just done.*)

SO THERE IT IS.

THE BOY IS SKILLED

I REALLY THINK THAT...

I MIGHT GET KILLED.

OR COULD THIS ACTU'LLY BE THE MOMENT

WHEN THE FORCES ARE BEGINNING TO ALIGN?

COULD THIS BE MINE?

IT'S MINE...

I'M GONNA SAVE THE GIRL...

> *(He goes inside the building, on top of the world.)*

> *(Then **VIC** emerges just as **CHARLOTTE** enters, heading home after work, holding a very full grocery bag along with an unwieldy backpack and briefcase.)*

VIC. Mizz Branson.

CHARLOTTE. Oh. Hi, Mr. Costello.

VIC. That boy of yours...

CHARLOTTE. *(Sigh.)* What did he do?

VIC. Nothing. He's very creative, huh? Always with the drawing.

CHARLOTTE. Creative he is.

VIC. Was his dad like that?

> *(This stops **CHARLOTTE**. She's never had a serious conversation with her surly landlord before.)*

CHARLOTTE. Yeah. He was in his way.

VIC. How so, if you don't mind me asking?

CHARLOTTE. My husband Mitch grew up on comic books, always loved them. Simon too. They couldn't get enough of it... Especially Sub-Mariner. He's kind of obscure, but they were obsessed.

VIC. Sub-Mariner, sure. He's great. Yeah, some folks prefer Aquaman, but he's such a pussy, right? What's great about Sub-Mariner is that he's sort of a villain and hero at the same time. Very complicated guy.

CHARLOTTE. God, the way they talked. It's like they had a secret language I never learned.

VIC. Fathers and sons.

CHARLOTTE. And Simon still has so many crazy ideas I can barely keep up.

VIC. Like what?

CHARLOTTE. Like he thinks the bus driver's a superhero. Or a supervillain or something.

VIC. Jim? The bus driver here?

CHARLOTTE. Yeah, I know, right.

VIC. Stranger things...

CHARLOTTE. What?

VIC. Who knows about people?

CHARLOTTE. Well, I'm pretty sure he's not a superhero.

    (*A beat.*)

VIC. Yeah. You're probably right.

    (**JIM** *emerges from the building.*)

    (**CHARLOTTE** *laughs when she sees him.*)

JIM. What?

CHARLOTTE. Nothing. Just... Freaky coincidences, right?

    (*An amused glance to* **VIC**. *Then* **VIC** *goes.*)

JIM. Sure... (*Re: her grocery bags.*) ...You want help with those?

CHARLOTTE. I'm good.

JIM. ...All that food. You must be a good cook.

CHARLOTTE. I'm overcompensating. I'm a lousy cook. And it's even worse when I try to get "creative." Thus the quinoa and kale tonight.

JIM. I've never had quinoa. Is it like rice?

CHARLOTTE. Sort of.

JIM. You know they make rice in a bag you can just microwave... I'm sort of a master of microwave cookery. I went through a very brief phase where I tried to cook. I bought a cookbook and tried to make this Cajun thing, with like nineteen ingredients. Followed the recipe, dirtied every pot and pan I had... But, end of the day, cooking for one...you know what I mean?... Well, good night.

> *(He starts to go.)*

CHARLOTTE. *(Suddenly.)* Hey, why don't you come over for dinner tonight? With me and Simon. Try the quinoa.

JIM. Oh...

CHARLOTTE. I've told you I'm a lousy cook, so expectations are low.

JIM. I...that's really nice. I'm not... Well, I'm not that used to eating with other people.

CHARLOTTE. Do you have like weird table manners?

JIM. I've been alone a long time.

> (**CHARLOTTE**'s *struck by this sudden flash of honesty from him, of vulnerability.*)

CHARLOTTE. Oh.

JIM. You get used to things, right?

CHARLOTTE. You do... Don't worry about it. I was just –

JIM. Yes. I'd like to come over for dinner. Thanks.

CHARLOTTE. Great. In about an hour then? Apartment 2D.

JIM. You got it. You need me to bring anything?

CHARLOTTE. Just a strong stomach.

JIM. Oh, that I have.

(*He smiles and goes.*)

(**CHARLOTTE** *stands frozen for a moment, a little shocked at her sudden invitation.*)

[MUSIC NO. 11 "THE MAN IN 4B (REPRISE 2)"]

Scene Seven
Charlotte and Simon's Apartment /
Fire Escape / The Roof

(About an hour later. **CHARLOTTE** *and* **SIMON**
are making dinner / setting the table.)

*(We see the fire escape outside their apartment
leading up to the roof.)*

SIMON.

I MEAN BOLD

CHARLOTTE.

YUP. I JUST SAID IT.

SIMON.

IMPRESSIVE

CHARLOTTE.

DO YOU THINK HE THINKS THAT IT'S A DATE?

SIMON.

MOM, OF COURSE HE THINKS THAT IT'S A DATE.

CHARLOTTE.

WHO CARES? I CARE. OH WELL, TOO LATE.
(Spoken in rhythm.) SHIT.

SIMON. *(Spoken in rhythm.)*

MOM, QUIT IT.
(Sung.) YOU KNOW YOU'RE GONNA BLOW THE WHOLE
THING IF YOU ACT LIKE THIS

CHARLOTTE.

THERE IS NO "THING." IT'S JUST A DATE – MEAL!
I'M A MESS!

SIMON.

YOU'LL BE FINE.

CHARLOTTE.

I HATE THIS DRESS

SIMON.
DRINK LOTS OF WINE.

CHARLOTTE.
I SHOULD CANCEL.

SIMON. *(Spoken in rhythm.)*
YOU *CAN'T* CANCEL.

CHARLOTTE. *(Spoken in rhythm.)*
SIMON PLEASE –

(A beat.)

SIMON. Mom. It'll be nice to have some company.

CHARLOTTE.
KEEP STIRRING, IT'S ALMOST DONE.

SIMON.
HOW MUCH LONGER? I REALLY HAVE TO RUN.

CHARLOTTE. *(Spoken in rhythm.)*
WHAT?!

SIMON. Sorry, I have to go to the library, so you're solo.

CHARLOTTE. No way!

SIMON. Mom, Selina Kyle does not seduce Batman with her son along.

CHARLOTTE. Okay, number one, I'm not seducing anyone, and number two, shut up.

SIMON. I have to do some research for my project. Vee's depending on me.

CHARLOTTE. He's going to think I lured him here.

SIMON. You did.

CHARLOTTE. Don't!

SIMON. And remember, the whole point is to ask him questions. Dig around a little. Pump him!

CHARLOTTE. I will not!

SIMON. *(Grabs his backpack.)* See you later. Don't poison
   him.

> *(He exits the apartment...)*

> *(But he immediately goes to the fire escape so
> he can secretly observe what's going on in the
> apartment. Peeks through a window.)*

CHARLOTTE. *(To herself.)* ...Who the hell is Selina Kyle??

[MUSIC NO. 12 "THE ADVENTURES OF THE AMAZING SEA-MARINER (REPRISE 2)"]

SIMON.
> NO ONE KNOWS THE SEA MARINER'S SECRET IDENTITY
> WHO HE IS – AND WHERE HE'S FROM
> BUT HE'S BOUND TO SLIP UP AT SOME POINT!
> AND TONIGHT...
> PERHAPS...
> THAT TIME HAS COME...

> *(The doorbell rings.)*

CHARLOTTE. Just a minute!

> *(She quickly straightens her dress, fluffs her
> hair, and goes to answer the door in a bit of
> a flurry.)*

> *(JIM enters. He's wearing a tie.)*

Hi!

JIM. Hey. I didn't feel right not bringing anything.

> *(He hands her a bag of uncooked microwave
> popcorn. A charming gesture.)*

That's the big bag, you know, with the real fake butter.

CHARLOTTE. Wow. Great. Come in.

JIM. Nice place! You have a view.

> (**SIMON** *ducks back as* **JIM** *looks out the window... He takes in the books all over the apartment.*)

Look at all these books.

CHARLOTTE. Curse of my trade... Well, make yourself at home. Shove some dead poets out of the way and take a seat. Dinner's almost ready.

> (*They're both nervous / excited. It's awkward and sweet and adult... She pours wine.*)

Red okay?

JIM. Sure.

CHARLOTTE. Oh, sorry, I didn't even ask if you drink.

JIM. Yeah, I do – but not too much! I'm not "a drinker," you know. I don't have a "problem." Just. Well. Sorry. Yeah, red is great... Where's your son?

CHARLOTTE. He's out tonight.

JIM. Oh.

CHARLOTTE. (*Quickly.*) I mean I didn't know he was going out, I thought he was going to be here, but then he told me he had plans. He's just down the street at the library, so he's still here, but he's not, you know, here-here... Sit down, please.

> (*She brings food to the table and they sit. They eat during:*)

JIM. This looks great.

CHARLOTTE. Thanks... Try the famous quinoa.

JIM. (*He tries it.*) It's...wow...like rice. But good rice. Really good rice.

[MUSIC NO. 13 "HOW DO YOU DO THIS AGAIN?"]

CHARLOTTE.   First time making it, so it's a little experimental. I put nutmeg in it, which isn't in the recipe. But you can't go wrong with nutmeg, can you? Or maybe you can. I don't know...

JIM.

> HOW DO YOU DO THIS AGAIN?
> BE CAUTIOUS BUT ENGAGE.
> IT'S FUNNY BUT I CAN'T RECALL WHEN
> I'VE HAD TO ACT MY AGE.
> AND DOES SHE EVEN KNOW
> HOW LONG IT'S BEEN SINCE I
> FELT THE NEED TO WEAR A TIE?

CHARLOTTE. ...But I'm no expert on nutmeg. Why am I so obsessed with nutmeg?

JIM.

> HOW CAN YOU CHANGE WHO YOU'VE BEEN?
> HOW CAN YOU PRETEND?
> YOU SWORE NOT TO LET SOMEONE IN
> BUT THEN YOU MAKE A FRIEND...
>
> AND ALL YOU'VE COME TO KNOW
> FEELS SOMEHOW OUT OF DATE
> ALL THIS, AND IT'S ONLY TEN TO EIGHT.

CHARLOTTE. How's the wine?

JIM. Really good. But I'm no expert. I'm more of a beer-in-front-of-the-TV-guy. Only I don't like beer. And I don't have a TV.

CHARLOTTE.

> HOW DO YOU DO THIS AGAIN?
> I THOUGHT I WAS PREPARED.
> CLOSE MY EYES. TAKE A BREATH. COUNT TO TEN.
> NO REASON TO BE SCARED...
> BUT SOMETHING'S OPENED UP.

I'VE NOTICED THERE'S A SHIFT.

LORD KNOWS, I COULD USE A LITTLE LIFT.

JIM.

HOW I'VE LONGED FOR EASY CONVERSATION

CHARLOTTE.

NERVOUS THAT I MIGHT SAY SOMETHING STRANGE

CHARLOTTE & JIM.

I NEVER THOUGHT I'D HAVE ANOTHER NIGHT LIKE THIS

AND IT'S NICE TO BE WRONG FOR A CHANGE...

JIM. Your son seems like a great kid.

CHARLOTTE. He is. A really great kid...

> (**SIMON,** *watching on the fire escape, is touched.*)

I just hope I'm a good mother. Sometimes it feels like I've spent the last two years living for Simon. And I don't think it's helping him, or me...

JIM. How do you mean?

CHARLOTTE. I keep telling myself to get moving, finish my book, start living my own life – but this is my life... So every night I go to bed thinking about all the things I could have done better. I go through the list in my head. All the failures along the way.

JIM. I know the feeling... You know I was nervous about coming tonight. I don't talk much to other people. "Loner" I guess you'd say. That's what people say. I just say "private"... But sometimes you start thinking... maybe it would be nice to have someone...

TO TALK TO

CHARLOTTE.

TO TRY WITH

JIM.

COME HOME TO

CHARLOTTE.
AND CRY WITH

JIM.
SHARE SECRETS

CHARLOTTE.
NO SECRETS

JIM.
GIVE UP THE BURDEN

CHARLOTTE.
SHARE THE BURDEN OF THIS LIFE...

JIM.
OF ALL THOSE PEOPLE...

CHARLOTTE.
THIS LONELY LIFE...

JIM.
OF HEARING ALL THOSE PEOPLE...

CHARLOTTE.
NOT ALONE...

JIM.
NOT ALONE...

CHARLOTTE & JIM.
ANYMORE

JIM. You know something... I don't even know your name.

CHARLOTTE. Charlotte. After *Charlotte's Web*.

JIM. That's a beautiful book.

CHARLOTTE. But a little sad.

JIM. Life is like that. Can't have one without the other.

CHARLOTTE. You think?

JIM. Beauty, sadness. That's the whole deal... *(He looks at her.)* ...Your name's perfect.

CHARLOTTE & JIM.

> HOW LONG HAVE I LIVED IN ISOLATION?
> LONGING TO CONNECT BUT OUT OF RANGE
> I THOUGHT THAT NO ONE HEARD ME OUT THERE IN THE
> WORLD
> AND IT'S NICE TO BE WRONG FOR A CHANGE
> IT'S NICE TO BE WRONG FOR A CHANGE.

> **[MUSIC NO. 14 "YOU DON'T KNOW WHAT I
> KNOW (REPRISE)"]**

> *(Then...**JIM** stops.)*

> *(He hears a musical sound in his head, a
> sharp tonality... **CHARLOTTE** doesn't hear it...
> Something changes in him. He's suddenly
> tense. Like he's having a panic attack.)*

> *(**SIMON** leans in, attentive, watching closely.)*

A VOICE.

> HELP ME...

ANOTHER VOICE.

> HELP ME...

TWO VOICES.

> HELP ME...

ANOTHER TWO VOICES.

> HELP ME...

SIMON.

> WHO'S THE MAN IN 4B...?

A VOICE.

> HELP ME...

JIM.

> YOU DON'T KNOW WHAT I KNOW...

SIMON.

> WHO'S THE MAN IN 4B...?

MORE VOICES.

> HELP ME...

CHARLOTTE. Are you okay...?

JIM. I'm sorry. I have to go.

CHARLOTTE. What do you mean go...?

JIM. I'm sorry. Dammit. I have to –

CHARLOTTE. Jim...!

> (JIM *bolts up and runs out of the apartment. Running up the stairs to the roof, in turmoil.*)

> (CHARLOTTE *sits there, mystified and hurt.*)

> (SIMON *watches from the fire escape as...*)

> (JIM *bursts through the door of the roof and dives into the air – transforming in midair – shimmering into a strange, spectral light, a powerful energy force, and zooming away into the night! Voices continue to sing "Help me" variously under the action.*)

SIMON.	JIM.	VOICES.
	YOU DON'T KNOW WHAT	HELP ME...
I	I –	
KNOW,	YOU DON'T KNOW WHAT	HELP ME...
I	I –	
KNOW!	YOU DON'T KNOW WHAT	HELP ME
I KNOW!	I KNOW	

> (SIMON *is stunned.*)

SIMON. *(Spoken in rhythm.)*
WOW...!

VOICES.
> OOH
> OOH

ACT II

Scene Eight
The Roof

(About an hour later.)

(SIMON and JIM are talking.)

SIMON. Can you walk through walls?

JIM. No.

SIMON. Do you have a Fortress of Solitude?

JIM. No.

SIMON. Do you have a secret cave?

JIM. No.

SIMON. Do you have a super kickass car?

JIM. No.

SIMON. Do you have a sidekick?

JIM. No.

SIMON. Do you want one?!

JIM. No! ...Let me make it simple: it's absolutely nothing

like any superhero comic book, or video game, or anything else you ever saw, ever.

SIMON. You're great at telling me what you're *not* – so what the hell are you?

JIM. I'm not supposed to talk about it.

SIMON. Yeah, well, you're not supposed to let people see you turn into an energy beam and fly away, are you?

(*Beat.*)

Don't you want to tell someone? Talk about it?

JIM. I've never talked about it...

(JIM *hesitates, looks at him.* SIMON *is so sincere.*)

I'm from another planet.

SIMON. I knew it!!

JIM. (*Shushes him.*) Shhh... My home world is beyond this galaxy. The beings from my planet are dispatched to other worlds to help those in need. It's our calling, our only purpose for existence. We assume the appearance of the people native to the planet, but we're invulnerable to any injury. Once we leave our home world we can never return, and we go alone.

(SIMON *stares, rapt.*)

SIMON. Holy. Shit.

JIM. Yeah.

SIMON. Holy...shit.

JIM. Okay, it sounds crazy when I say it out loud.

SIMON. I believe you. I mean I saw you...you know... (*He makes a "flying" gesture and sound.*) ...What was that I saw?

JIM. Transforming from this identity to my essential energy... And I wish you hadn't seen any of it!

SIMON. You're not going to zap my memory, are you?

JIM. Do you think we'd be having this conversation if I could?

SIMON. How do you know when people need you? Do you have like a bat-signal or something?

JIM. I sort of hear the voices in my head – the people in need.

SIMON. Okay, so tonight – were you going to battle your super-villain archnemesis?

JIM. No. I was trying to stop a bus crash in Honduras.

SIMON. *(Disappointed, sobered.)* Really?

JIM. Yes. Really.

> *(Beat.)*

SIMON. So, what happened?

JIM. I saved half of them.

> *(SIMON didn't expect this. Looks at him... Sees the pain in JIM's eyes.)*

[MUSIC NO. 16 "IT'S NOT LIKE IN THE MOVIES"]

That's what it's really like. You save half of them. If you're lucky... My life's not what you think, Simon.

NO ONE CAN GET TOO CLOSE
NO ONE CAN GET INSIDE OF YOU
NO ONE CAN KNOW THE SECRETS THAT YOU KEEP
YOUR HEAD IS ALWAYS DOWN
HOPING THAT PEOPLE SLIDE PAST YOU
ALMOST AS IF YOU'RE WALKING IN YOUR SLEEP
AND YOU CAN'T CRY

THOUGH YOU HURT
YOU ARE ALWAYS, ON ALERT
AND THOUGH YOU TRY, AND YOU FLY, PEOPLE DIE.

IT'S NOT LIKE IN THE MOVIES
WHERE THE HERO IS LOVED AND KNOWN
IT'S NOT LIKE IN THE MOVIES
I SPEND MY DAYS ALONE
I DON'T EVEN GET A HUG
FROM THE KID STUCK IN THE TREE
IT'S NOT LIKE IN THE MOVIES
NO ONE KNOWS IT'S ME.

YOU DON'T DRIVE A TRICKED-OUT CAR

    (Beat.)

YOU DON'T WORK AT A LAB OR THE *DAILY*...??

SIMON. *Planet*?

JIM. Right.

FOR A BOSS WHO YELLS, BUT HAS A HEART OF GOLD
YOU DON'T BLEED, OR SCRAPE, OR SCAR
WELL, AT LEAST NOT ON THE OUTSIDE
AND YOU'RE AT YOUR PEAK, BUT YOU CAN'T HELP
    FEELING OLD

YOU'RE ALWAYS TIRED, BUT YOU CAN'T REST
YOU OFTEN LOSE, THOUGH YOU'VE DONE YOUR BEST
THERE'S NO PARADE, NO CITY KEY, JUST ANONYMITY

IT'S NOT LIKE IN THE MOVIES
IT'S A LITTLE MORE COMPLEX
IT'S NOT LIKE IN THE MOVIES
NO CGI EFFECTS
I DON'T GET TO LEARN "LIFE LESSONS" FROM MY HUMAN
    FAMILY
IT'S NOT LIKE IN THE MOVIES
NO ONE KNOWS IT'S ME
I'VE TRIED TO WALK AWAY

SO I WON'T WAKE EACH DAY
TO CRIES OF ANGUISH IN MY HEAD
BUT IF I DISAPPEAR
YOU'LL ALL IMPLODE, *THAT'S* CLEAR
IT'S GOTTEN WORSE AND WORSE WITH EV'RY PASSING
    YEAR...

I DON'T MEAN TO SOUND SO HARSH
I'VE ALSO SEEN THE GOOD OUT THERE
EMPATHY AND KINDNESS ON DISPLAY
BUT EV'RY TIME I THINK I CAN
RELEASE MYSELF FROM THIS NIGHTMARE
SOMEONE TRIES TO BLOW THE WORLD AWAY.

SO, I DON'T WANT TO SOUND INSINCERE
BUT I THINK YOU SHOULD JUST FORGET WHAT
    HAPPENED HERE
'CAUSE NO ONE EVER TRULY SEES ME.

SIMON. *(Spoken in rhythm.)*
YOU'RE JIM, THE MAN IN 4B.

JIM.
NOW SIMON THAT'S AN ENDING I WOULD REALLY LIKE
    TO SEE.
BUT I CAN'T MAKE A LIFE OUT OF MY SECRET IDENTITY.

SIMON. Why not?
IT'S NOT LIKE IN THE MOVIES...

I have to go. My mom will be looking for me... Don't
worry. Your secret's safe.

    (He goes.)

JIM.
NO ONE KNOWS IT'S ME.

Scene Nine
Charlotte and Simon's Apartment

[MUSIC NO. 17 "THE MAN IN 4B (REPRISE 3)"]

(SIMON *enters.*)

(CHARLOTTE *is working on her laptop, making notes for her book.*)

CHARLOTTE.
HOW WAS YOUR EVENING?

SIMON.
GREAT.
I THINK THAT MY PROJECT IS COMING ALONG REAL WELL.
HOW WAS YOUR "DATE"?

CHARLOTTE.
NOT GREAT. IT KIND OF WENT TO HELL.

SIMON. *(Spoken in rhythm.)*
WHAT HAPPENED?

CHARLOTTE.
HE PANICKED. THEN WALKED OUT. NO RAN OUT. BOLTED. WHOOSH. AWAY HE FLEW.
I JUST KNEW...

SIMON.
WELL, MAYBE HE GOT SICK FROM THE QUINOA, OR SOMETHING

CHARLOTTE.
HE WAS FINE. IT WAS FINE. THEN IT WASN'T.
I EMBARRASSED MYSELF I'M SURE.

SIMON.
MOM, THAT'S WHAT A FIRST DATE IS FOR.

CHARLOTTE. *(Spoken in rhythm.)*

OH REALLY?

(Sung.) WELL IF THAT'S THE CASE I TAKE FIRST PLACE

YOU SHOULD HAVE SEEN THE LOOK OF HORROR ON HIS FACE!

OH, SIMON, THIS WAS CLEARLY A MISTAKE.

SIMON.

MOM. GIVE YOURSELF A BREAK.

HE WAS PROBABLY SICK...

CHARLOTTE.

PROBABLY SICK...

(She exits.)

*(Music as **SIMON** steps forward and excitedly imagines a new story.)*

[MUSIC NO. 18 "THE AMAZING ADVENTURES OF THE SEA-MARINER (REPRISE 3)"]

SIMON.

JUST WHEN YOU THINK THERE ARE NO MORE SURPRISES

A NEW CHARACTER LEAPS INTO THE FRAY.

Why it's the Sea-Mariner's handsome and very athletic young sidekick!

NEWT MINNOW!

(The name's an epic fail.)

Name to come.

AND TOGETHER, THESE TWO WILL SAVE THE DAY...

(And we are at...)

Scene Ten
The Building

(Almost evening.)

*(**SIMON** and **VEE** wander on.)*

SIMON. ...I'm not sure exactly how it's going to turn out, but I think my project's pretty cool so far. I mean when you really start thinking about it, it's kind of inspiring. How would you change the world?

VEE. And I was thinking, if we only have a hundred years until the world ends, like really ends...what would you do that day?

SIMON. The last day on Earth? Like before the rocket ships take us to our colony on Alderaan.

VEE. Where?

SIMON. Princess Leia's home planet. Duh.

VEE. Doesn't that get destroyed?

SIMON. So maybe we won't go there... You know if Superman were here, he could save the world. That's like his job description.

VEE. *(Smiles.)* Too bad he's not real.

SIMON. *(Secret smile.)* Yeah, too bad.

(They stroll for a beat.)

VEE. So what if it really was the last day on earth... What would you do...?

SIMON. There's a cheery thought...

[MUSIC NO. 19 "IF I ONLY HAD ONE DAY"]

What about you?

VEE.

> IF I ONLY HAD ONE DAY
> IF I ONLY HAD ONE DAY
> I'D WAKE UP AND THROW MY TOOTHBRUSH AWAY
> AND THEN I'D BINGE ON ICE CREAM.
> *(Spoken in rhythm.)* THE PERFECT BREAKFAST,
> *(Sung.)* WOULDN'T YOU SAY?

SIMON. I would.

VEE.

> IF I ONLY HAD ONE DAY.

> Your turn!

SIMON.

> IF I ONLY HAD ONE DAY
> BEFORE IT ALL GOES WRONG
> I'D SPEND THE DAY WITH EV'RY BEATLES SONG.

VEE. Nice.

SIMON.

> THOUGH PROB'LY NOT THEIR SOLO STUFF, I MEAN IT'S
>   FINE, JUST NOT AS STRONG...

VEE. Wow.

SIMON.

> IF I ONLY HAD ONE DAY

VEE.

> IF I ONLY HAD ONE DAY
> I WOULD TAKE SOME TIME ALONE
> SO I COULD READ THE FINAL PAGE OF EV'RY BOOK I OWN
> OH! THEN LATER DO A VICT'RY DANCE AS I ANNIHILATE
>   MY PHONE
> IF I ONLY HAD ONE DAY

SIMON & VEE.

> THERE'S JUST NO WAY TO GET TO EV'RYTHING
> WITH JUST ONE DAY, SOMETHING HAS TO GIVE.

VEE.

BUT SEEING WHAT'S BEEN DEALT, THAT THIS WORLD'S
    ABOUT TO MELT
I WOULD FIND A WAY TO TRULY LIVE
I'D LIVE
SO IF I ONLY HAD ONE DAY
I'D TAKE MY LITTLE DOG
AND FIND A BEACH WHERE WE COULD RUN AND PLAY
AND THEN I'D WATCH THE SUNSET,
AND THEN WATCH IT FADE AWAY...
IF I ONLY HAD ONE DAY.

(They exit.)

*(As **CHARLOTTE** emerges and sits on the steps, relaxing with a cup of coffee as she reads another heavily-notated volume of John Clare poetry.)*

*(**VIC** emerges from the building.)*

VIC. *(Re: her book of poetry.)* Jeez, that's a book and a half.

CHARLOTTE. Oh, hey... Yeah. It's work: publish or perish.

VIC. All those little words, I'd get a headache. Whattaya you sitting out here working anyway? Friday evening, you oughta be out dancing or something.

CHARLOTTE. *(Smiles.)* Oh, my dancing days are behind me I think.

VIC. What a thing to say. That's an awful thing. You're a beautiful lady who reads big books, this is a desirable thing I would think in the circles you run in.

CHARLOTTE. I don't really run in any circles these days. Too busy trying to keep my job and take care of Simon and... *(Beat.)* ...It's just a bad time.

VIC. ...You know what was hardest for me? The obituary. Writing the obituary.

*(**CHARLOTTE** looks at him.)*

Lost my wife seven years ago, God rest her soul. So I wanted to write an obituary for the parish newspaper... What do you say? How do you pick those words?... Worst weeks of my life trying to figure that out: how to say goodbye... But you got to do it, yeah?

CHARLOTTE. For me it's the tombstone. What do we say about him? It's been two years, but I just can't seem to do it.

VIC. Good time, bad time, still gotta get on with your life, right?

CHARLOTTE. Someday.

VIC. Someday's never... Your son. He was with him when it happened? He saw the accident?

CHARLOTTE. Yeah.

VIC. What a thing to see.

CHARLOTTE. And when he thinks about Mitch – I'm afraid that's all he sees. That's in his head all the time... So he won't talk about his dad at all. Made me take down all the pictures of him. That was the worst.

VIC. No wonder he loves comic books...

*(**CHARLOTTE** looks at him. He explains.)*

The hero always comes back... Enjoy this fine evening, Mizz Branson.

(He goes.)

*(**JIM** emerges from the building, practically running into **CHARLOTTE**.)*

JIM. Okay, first person I see. Cool.

CHARLOTTE. Well, well, well, well.

JIM. All right. I'm an idiot, I'm sorry. I'm so sorry. Last night was great, really great and I... There's no excuse. Please forgive me.

CHARLOTTE. So...what happened?

JIM. I can't explain.

CHARLOTTE. I think you should try.

JIM. I have panic attacks sometimes. Like anxiety. It's embarrassing. I never know when they're going to come. I do meditation, I do controlled breathing but... they just happen and I have to go. So I don't go out much.

>*(He's quiet, vulnerable.)*

...Last night was a big step for me.

CHARLOTTE. For me too.

>*(**SIMON** and **VEE** stroll on for a moment, talking quietly.)*

JIM. Wow, look at them... Is that the girl he likes?

CHARLOTTE. Yeah.

>*(**SIMON** and **VEE** wander off.)*

It's like I can suddenly see his whole future. Marriage and kids. God, I don't want to lose him. Or I constantly want to get rid of him. One or the other.

>*(**JIM** smiles.)*

I used to walk him to school, holding his hand. I remember the day he got old enough that he let go of my hand. I had to let him cross the street by himself. I was so scared for him... You want to protect them all the time... But you can't. You can't.

JIM. They get hurt. Everyone does... Can you give me another chance? Let me make dinner for you and Simon. My microwave is *so* ready.

CHARLOTTE. Simon would like that.

JIM. Oh?

CHARLOTTE. Don't laugh but...he thinks you're a superhero.

(A frozen beat. Then **JIM** *laughs.)*

JIM. Unmasked!

(They laugh.)

CHARLOTTE. He's all about comics and superheroes. He draws them and it makes him so happy.

JIM. Nothing wrong with believing in something, is there?

CHARLOTTE. Jim, I appreciate what you said, but this is just a rough time for us, okay? It's not you.

JIM. Maybe I could help... Please. Let me try.

CHARLOTTE. It's difficult right now.

[MUSIC NO. 20 "IN BETWEEN"]

My son needs me. And my students need me. And I don't have tenure. When Mitch was alive I could handle it all somehow...

DO YOU EVER FEEL LIKE YOU'VE LOST WHO YOU WERE?
YOU EXAMINE YOUR LIFE AND NOTHING MAKES SENSE
DAYS, WEEKS AND MONTHS, THEY GO BY IN A BLUR
AND YOU CANNOT FIND THE PRESENT TENSE.

I'M NEEDED AT HOME. I'M NEEDED AT WORK.
BUT WHEREVER I AM, I'M NOT REALLY THERE
AND ANY INDULGENCE MAKES ME FEEL LIKE A JERK.
I GIVE UP ON DREAMS AND TRY NOT TO CARE.

IT'S A LIFELONG STRUGGLE
FOR A BALANCE I'VE NEVER SEEN.
THE UNWINNABLE FIGHT
BUT IT'S NOT BLACK OR WHITE
IT'S IN BETWEEN.

JIM.

> EACH DAY I WAKE WITH A FEELING OF DREAD
> SCARED OF THE TRIALS THAT AWAIT
> AND ALL OF THESE VOICES THAT SCREAM IN MY HEAD
> TELLING ME THAT IT'S TOO LATE.
>
> 'CAUSE MY FATE WAS SEALED A LONG TIME AGO
> THIS IS MY LIFE, FOR BETTER OR WORSE,
> AND TO TELL YOU THE TRUTH, I DON'T REALLY KNOW
> IF I'M A BLESSING OR A CURSE.
>
> SO I STARE AT THE WRECKAGE
> I JUST CAN'T LEAVE THE SCENE
> AND THERE'S NO END IN SIGHT
> 'CAUSE IT'S NOT BLACK OR WHITE
> IT'S IN BETWEEN
> I USED TO THINK I HAD IT ALL FIGURED OUT

CHARLOTTE.

> I USED TO THINK I HAD IT ALL FIGURED OUT

JIM.

> I WOULD JUST ACCEPT THE WAY THINGS ARE

CHARLOTTE.

> THE WAY THINGS ARE...

JIM & CHARLOTTE.

> BUT AT THE END OF THE DAY
> THERE HAS TO BE A WAY TO FIND SOME PEACE
> THOUGH THEY'LL SAY I'VE COME UP SHORT
> I'LL RELEASE MYSELF FROM ALL THAT THEY DISTORT
> AND THEN, MAYBE...
> I'LL FIND ME.

CHARLOTTE.

> MAYBE IT'S TIME TO CUT MYSELF SLACK
> TO LOOK AT MY LIFE AND HIT RESET

JIM.

> MAYBE IT'S TIME TO PULL MYSELF BACK
> AND LIVE WITHOUT REGRET

JIM & CHARLOTTE.
>IT'S THE ENDLESS STRUGGLE
>TO WIPE THE SLATE CLEAN
>AND THEN MAYBE I MIGHT
>GIVE IN, AND NOT FIGHT
>'CAUSE IT'S NOT BLACK OR WHITE
>IT'S IN BETWEEN.

>>*(Easily, gently...they kiss.)*

>>*(Just as **SIMON** and **VEE** enter. He stares, shocked and pleased.)*

SIMON. No...way.

VEE. What?

SIMON. *(Nods.)* That's my mom.

VEE. Go Simon's mom! ...Hey, I have to go. See you at school.

SIMON. You bet. Thanks for...talking to me.

>>*(**VEE** smiles and goes.)*

>>*(Meanwhile, **CHARLOTTE** gathers up her books and things as **JIM** goes to **SIMON** and they talk privately.)*

SIMON. You and my mom. Nice moves.

JIM. *(Smiles.)* Hey, I'm supposed to be fearless, right?

SIMON. So what's on for tonight? A little, you know, zooming around?

JIM. Yeah, there's this Superhero bar I like to go to.

>>*(**SIMON** laughs.)*

SIMON. You should take me with you some time. You totally need a sidekick.

JIM. Oh, you think you're ready for that?

SIMON. Man, I was practically born in the bat cave.

(**CHARLOTTE** *approaches.*)

JIM. Have a good night, guys. I'm glad we talked.

CHARLOTTE. Me too. 'Night.

(**JIM** *goes.*)

(**CHARLOTTE** *and* **SIMON** *are left alone onstage.*)

[MUSIC NO. 20A "MY DAD, THE SUPERHERO INTRO"]

SIMON. So...I guess you decided to give him another chance.

CHARLOTTE. Simon, this doesn't mean anything big, it's just –

SIMON. Mom, I totally get it... Like I said, he's pretty special, huh? Pretty...superheroic.

CHARLOTTE. Oh that. Right... In his own way, he kinda is.

SIMON. I'll be up in a second, okay?

CHARLOTTE. Sure.

(*She goes inside.*)

(**SIMON** *starts imagining it. Trying a new comic book idea on for size.*)

SIMON. "My Mom and the Superhero"... Could be... "My Mom and her Super Boyfriend"... No...

(*Then it comes to him.*)

[MUSIC NO. 21 "MY DAD, THE SUPERHERO"]

MY DAD, THE SUPERHERO
MY DAD, THE STAR.

MY DAD, THE BOLT OF LIGHTNING
SENT TO US FROM FAR AWAY...
WON'T YOU STAY WITH US?

YOU'LL COME TO OUR RESCUE
WHEN HOPE SEEMS LOST.
TO SHIELD AND PROTECT US
NO MATTER WHAT THE COST MIGHT BE...
JUST THE THREE OF US.
AND YOU'LL NEVER DIE.
YOU'LL NEVER DIE.

MY DAD, THE SUPERHERO
MIGHT MISS A GAME
BUT I WON'T SPEND ANOTHER BIRTHDAY
CRYING ALL THE SAME SAD TEARS
THERE'LL BE CHEERS OF JOY.

MAYBE I COULD GO WITH YOU TO WORK ONE DAY?
YOU COULD TEACH ME THE BUS'NESS
I WON'T GET IN THE WAY, YOU'LL SEE
I CAN BE YOUR SUPER BOY.
AND YOU'LL NEVER DIE.
YOU'LL NEVER DIE.

AND OVER TIME OUR SPECIAL BOND WILL ONLY GROW.
I WON'T THINK ON THE THINGS THAT HAPPENED YEARS
    AGO!
IF IT'S LATE AT NIGHT
AND YOU'RE STILL NOT HOME,
I KNOW THAT YOU WILL BE ALL RIGHT.
I KNOW...
I KNOW.

MY DAD THE SUPERHERO
WILL LOVE MY MOM.
HE'LL MAKE HER FEEL SO SPECIAL
AND LIFE WILL BE SO CALM AND FREE...
JUST THE THREE OF US.
AND YOU'LL NEVER...

MY DAD THE SUPERHERO.
MY DAD THE SUPERHERO.
MY DAD THE SUPERHERO...

(**SIMON** *exits.*)

Scene Eleven
Charlotte and Simon's Apartment

(There's a passage of time.)

[MUSIC NO. 22 "IT HAPPENS TO YOU"]

*(**CHARLOTTE** is thinking about it all...)*

CHARLOTTE.

THE DAYS HAVE GENTLY PASSED.

THE WORLD FEELS SAFE AND NEW.

BUT WILL THIS FEELING LAST?

THERE IS STILL SO MUCH MYSTERY AROUND YOU...

WHAT IF YOU ARE THE THING THAT SIMON THINKS YOU ARE?

A SUPERHERO.

I MEAN IT'S CRAZY TO EVEN SAY THAT.

BUT LET'S JUST SAY FOR A MINUTE THAT IT'S TRUE.

WHAT COULD YOU DO? REALLY DO...?

COULD YOU FLY ME AROUND?

IT SURE IS FASTER.

TRAFFIC, A THING OF THE PAST.

MOVE AT THE SPEED OF SOUND TO HALT SOME DISASTER.

BUT GET HOME TO ME TWICE AS FAST!

WOULD YOU FEEL PAIN?

DO YOU GET COLD?

WILL YOU GROW OLD?

WOULD I EVEN NEED A JOB?

GOD THAT SOUNDS SO EXCITING!

WAIT A MINUTE, YES, I WOULD.

I MEAN YOU'RE STILL UNEMPLOYED.

OR IS YOUR JOB JUST A SIMPLE DISGUISE TO HIDE WHAT YOU'RE HIDING?

AND YOU'RE CONFIDING IN ME.

NATURALLY.

WOULD WE GO ON TRIPS, TAKE WALKS, SEE MOVIES?
WELL, NOT WHEN YOU'RE OUT FIGHTING CRIME.
THERE WOULD BE SOME ADJUSTMENTS, SOME THINGS
    TO GET USED TO.
BUT I KNOW THAT MOST OF THE TIME
YOU WOULD BE HERE,
EXCEPT WHEN YOU'RE NOT.
YOU MIGHT MISS A LOT.

AND WHAT ABOUT THE BEDROOM?
I'D BE SCARED TO DEATH OF THE BEDROOM
I'D BE HOLDING MY BREATH IN THE BEDROOM!
HOPING AND PRAYING IT'S EV'RYTHING I DREAMED IT
    WOULD BE!
A SUPERSONIC OTHERWORLDLY FEELING IN ME THAT
    WON'T EVER FADE...
THAT WON'T LET ME DOWN.
THAT WON'T GO AWAY AGAIN

AND WHAT ABOUT OUR SAFETY?
I KNOW THERE'LL BE DANGER,
WILL WE ALWAYS COME FIRST?
OR WILL THE BUBBLE SUDDENLY BURST?
WHEN WE WATCH YOU FLY AWAY INTO THIN AIR...?
ANOTHER DISAPPOINTMENT WE CAN'T BEAR
SO YOU REALLY HAVE TO PROMISE YOU'LL BE THERE.

YOU CAN'T, CAN YOU?
DON'T EVEN TRY TO CONVINCE ME
YOU'LL ONLY BE FOOLING US BOTH.
'CAUSE I'VE HEARD THAT BEFORE
THEN HE WALKED OUT THE DOOR
AND I NEVER SAW HIM AGAIN!
AND HOW MANY TIMES DOES THAT HAPPEN EACH DAY?
SOMEONE IS TAKEN AWAY.
IT'S A STORY YOU SEE ALL THE TIME ON THE NEWS.
BUT YOU NEVER THINK IT CAN HAPPEN TO YOU.
THEN IT HAPPENS TO YOU...

IT HAPPENS TO YOU...
EV'RY DAY IT KEEPS HAPP'NING TO YOU!

SO WHY GO THROUGH THAT HELL?
IT'S BEST NOT TO DWELL ON WHAT COULD BE –
WHAT *SHOULD* BE –
YOU'RE STUCK IN WHAT IS...
AND WHAT IS...
...IS...
LOST.
HELP ME...
HELP ME...

> *(This is agonizing for her.)*

> *(**SIMON** enters with the table set for dinner and food waiting. **CHARLOTTE** remains standing where she finished the song, tense, her emotions still roiling.)*

SIMON. Why are you so stressed out?! It's only fifteen minutes.

CHARLOTTE. It's not like it's the first time...

> *(And we are at...)*

Scene Twelve
Charlotte and Simon's Apartment

(Evening.)

SIMON. Mom, people get held up, it's no big deal...

(No answer from **CHARLOTTE.***)*

...Do you want me to read you some John Clare poems to calm down?

(Doorbell rings, he goes to answer it.)

Come on in.

JIM. Sorry I'm late, the trains were –

SIMON. Don't worry about it.

JIM. *(Kisses* **CHARLOTTE.***)* Sorry Charlotte. My job interview ran long and the trains were all messed up so I had to –

CHARLOTTE. It's okay, sit down.

(They sit to eat. She is preoccupied.)

SIMON. I made the meatballs and Mom made the asparagus thing. Such as it is.

JIM. Wow, it looks fantastic. So, you excited for your big presentation tomorrow?

SIMON. More like petrified.

JIM. Come on, it'll be great. I can't wait to see it. And I'm sure Vee'll love it.

CHARLOTTE. Only you're late a lot. I mean a few times now.

JIM. Yeah, I know. I just had a lot going on today. Sorry.

CHARLOTTE. Forget it. I'm just in a mood. Bad day at work. Mitch, could you pass the –? ...Sorry, Jim.

JIM. No problem... You know I was thinking, on my old
   bus route I passed this mini-golf course. It's off the
   expressway, but looks great. I thought maybe we could
   all go there next weekend?

SIMON. Mini-golf! Far out!

JIM. No, it looks really fun. You could ask Vee.

SIMON. The only thing – and I mean the only thing on
   the entire planet – that could possibly make me more
   un-cool in her eyes would be a mini-golf date.

JIM. What do you think, Charlotte?

CHARLOTTE. Next weekend? I don't know. I'll have to
   check. I think we have something.

SIMON. When do we ever have anything?

CHARLOTTE. Let me check, Simon.

SIMON. But it could be really –

CHARLOTTE. *(Too sharply.)* Simon. *Enough.*

   (Now there's tension. Discomfort.)

   (They eat in silence for a moment.)

   Is that a hobby of yours, golf?

JIM. What? No, not really.

CHARLOTTE. Do you have any hobbies?

JIM. I just saw it from the bus.

CHARLOTTE. I mean, we know so little about you...

JIM. Nothing to know really. I'm just boring.

CHARLOTTE. And you are late a lot. I know things happen
   and come up but it's not great sitting here wondering if
   you're okay. Where do you go all the time?

JIM. Nowhere, it's just –

CHARLOTTE. *(Snaps.)* It's like you're keeping secrets. *When are you going to be honest with us?*

SIMON. Mom...

CHARLOTTE. I'm sorry. I need a minute.

(She goes quickly.)

JIM. So...?

SIMON. Yeah.

JIM. This is totally not working.

SIMON. You gotta tell her.

JIM. No way.

SIMON. Come on, man, she needs to know. Otherwise you're gonna completely blow it with her! You're so goddamn mysterious it's freaking her out.

JIM. I don't think it's that.

SIMON. You need to tell her.

JIM. Simon, it's not that easy.

SIMON. *(Firmly.)* You know what, Jim, it's exactly that easy.

JIM. Look, if I start telling people what do you think happens? It'll be camera crews and helicopters and drones and spy cams and whatever else. It'll go viral in two seconds. Then I'm not anonymous. That means I can't do my job. That means people die.

SIMON. Don't put that on me! Just stop lying to my mom!

JIM. It's too dangerous.

SIMON. So you're afraid?

JIM. I don't want to hurt her or you or –

SIMON. This has nothing to do with us – this is all about you. Fine. Just zoom into a beam of light and fly away, right?

JIM. Look, I know this is hard. I know you're disappointed. But there are consequences to things and –

SIMON. Don't lecture me. You're not my dad. He's dead, remember? One of those people you *didn't* save. *Where were you that day, huh?!*

> (*His sudden bitterness is shocking.*)
>
> (*A beat.*)

JIM. I can't be everywhere, Simon. I have to make choices.

> (*He goes.*)
>
> (**SIMON** *pulls out his pad. Starts drawing angrily, with emotion.*)
>
> (**CHARLOTTE** *re-enters.*)

CHARLOTTE. Where's Jim?

SIMON. What was that all about?! It was really embarrassing.

CHARLOTTE. I just needed a second, okay?

SIMON. Well, it was rude. And I have work to do for my project –

CHARLOTTE. Simon. Sit down.

SIMON. (*Doesn't sit.*) This is about Jim, isn't it?

CHARLOTTE. Partly.

SIMON. You've got to give him a chance –

CHARLOTTE. Simon –

SIMON. Just give it a little more time –!

CHARLOTTE. *Simon. Listen to me...* I'm worried we're not ready.

SIMON. For what?

CHARLOTTE. For Jim. For someone like that in our lives.

SIMON. Mom – Mom – just stop. Listen to me for a second. This is going to sound crazy and I know you're not going to believe me, but you've got to try... I was right. Our whole thing about Jim, remember? ...He's... not like us.

CHARLOTTE. What do you mean?

SIMON. ...He's from another planet. Wait, I know! Just hear me out! He's from another planet and he has to help people so that's why he's late all the time and –

CHARLOTTE. Simon.

SIMON. Listen! I know Batman's not real, and Spiderman's not real, I know that, *but Jim is!*

CHARLOTTE. *Simon, enough.*

SIMON. Mom –

CHARLOTTE. This isn't about Jim. Or Superman. Or anyone else. *It's about Dad!* And none of this is going to get any better until you talk about him! I know it's hard, but I'm only thinking about what's best for you.

SIMON. No, you're not! You're thinking about *you*, like you always do! If you thought for one minute about me we wouldn't be living in this shithole, we would be in our old house, the house I loved, where I had friends at school, the house I grew up in, the house Dad lived in –

CHARLOTTE. I'm sorry!! All right?! I'm not perfect and I make mistakes and maybe moving here was one of them! I'm sure it was. But I couldn't live in that house anymore. He was everywhere and I just couldn't... But we can't just remove him from our lives. I'm so afraid if we don't talk about him, he really will be gone.

SIMON. Don't.

CHARLOTTE. Please. Tell me about that day. You went to the movies, was it good? Did he laugh? Did he tell those stupid jokes? What did you –?

SIMON. Stop it!

CHARLOTTE. Please trust me, if you talk about it, it will help.

SIMON. Jesus. You're constantly putting this on me – talk about him, tell me about the accident, get past it, make new friends, start living your life – *but what about you*?! You're stuck on that goddamn book and you haven't done anything about it or written a word and you never see people and when we finally meet someone nice you won't even give it a chance! It's like I don't have a dad *or* a mom anymore. *You're as dead as he is.*

> *(He goes.)*

> (**CHARLOTTE** *is stunned by his raw emotion.*)

Scene Thirteen
Graveyard

(Later that evening.)

*(**CHARLOTTE** stands alone at her husband's grave. There's no grave marker yet.)*

CHARLOTTE. Mitch... I need to talk about Simon... I need to talk about everything...

(Beat.)

So I'm dating a guy now I guess. Guy from the building. And Simon really likes him. That's what kills me. I'm so afraid he's going to get hurt if I do the wrong thing...

(Beat.)

And I have to figure out what goes on your tombstone. I've been thinking about it a lot... I spend my whole goddamn life around words, but I can't seem to pick these ones. I asked Simon to help me, but of course he won't talk about it...

[MUSIC NO. 23 "WHAT ARE THE WORDS?"]

But it's been so long now, and I know I just have to do it...

HOW DO I FIND THE WORDS TO SAY
WHEN THE THOUGHT OF IT JUST BREAKS MY HEART?
I COULD USE SOME GUIDANCE FROM YOU TODAY
TO HELP ME FIND THE COURAGE TO START.

HOW DO I SUMMARIZE YOUR LIFE
WHEN YOUR LIFE HAD JUST BEGUN?
"HONORED FATHER, HUSBAND, TO LOVING SON, AND
 WIFE.
THE VICTIM OF A TRAGIC HIT AND RUN"
SEE, THERE I GO AGAIN WITH FACTS AND FURY

THE KIND OF WORDS THAT SHOULD GIVE ME PAUSE
FOR THIS MAN FILLED OUR DAILY LIVES WITH POETRY
SO, HE NEEDS TO BE REMEMBERED AS HE WAS.
HE WAS NIGHT...
HE WAS DAY...
HE WAS SIGHT
THAT WAS TAKEN AWAY.
HELP ME...
I KNOW THAT I MUST MOVE ON.
I KNOW I MUST LET YOU GO
I MISS YOU SO...
SO HERE LIES THE MAN WHO MADE US LAUGH.
THE MAN WHO KEPT US SANE.
THE MAN WHO KNEW JUST WHAT TO DO.
THE MAN THAT I WAS MARRIED TO...
A SIMPLE WORD JUST CAME INTO VIEW
BELOVED.
YOU'RE BELOVED.
BELOVED.
AND I LOVED YOU.

Scene Fourteen
High School / Street

[MUSIC NO. 23A "HELP ME..."]

(The high school cafeteria, currently being set up for Vee's big Hundred Years event. Displays here and there. Signs: "100 Years to Save the Planet.")

*(**SIMON** is working on his laptop, which is attached to a projector. **VEE** goes to him.)*

VEE. *(Re: his project.)* So how's it going?

SIMON. Making the final adjustments now.

VEE. *(Tries to look at his laptop.)* You've been very secretive...

SIMON. No peeking.

VEE. Do you have anyone coming tonight?

SIMON. Just my family.

VEE. Great. See you later.

> *(She starts to go, stops.)*

Simon, thanks for helping out. You really saved the day.

> *(She smiles and moves on.)*

> *(**SIMON** continues to work on his laptop.)*

> *(Meanwhile...)*

> *(**CHARLOTTE** and **JIM** are walking to the school. They are both dressed up for Simon's big night. **JIM**'s wearing a tie.)*

CHARLOTTE. ...It was awful. He didn't even want me to come tonight.

JIM. Of course he did. He was just mad.

CHARLOTTE. I'm glad you're with me. I really appreciate you coming.

JIM. Anything I can do to help. That's why I'm here.

CHARLOTTE. Just being here is plenty. It'll mean a lot to Simon. And it does to me.

JIM. Does this mean mini-golf is back on?

(CHARLOTTE *laughs.*)

(JIM *suddenly stops.*)

(*As at the end of Act I, he hears a musical sound in his head, a sharp tonality...* CHARLOTTE *doesn't hear it... Something changes in* JIM. *He's suddenly tense. It's like a panic attack, agony escalating.*)

A VOICE.
    HELP ME...

JIM. I'm so sorry...

CHARLOTTE. What?

A VOICE.
    HELP ME...

JIM. It's happening. I can't breathe – I have to go –

CHARLOTTE. Can I help?

JIM. You don't know what this is like.

CHARLOTTE. Let me help, please. How can I –?

JIM. Goddamn it. I can't stay here –

VOICES. (*Singing under the following dialogue.*)
    HELP ME... HELP ME... HELP ME...

CHARLOTTE. No, Jim, *not tonight* –

JIM. I'm sorry. *Tell Simon I'm sorry.*

> *(He hurries off.)*
>
> *(**CHARLOTTE** stands for a moment, then goes and we're back to the high school...)*
>
> *(The Hundred Years event is underway.)*
>
> *(**CHARLOTTE** is watching. So too are **RACHEL** and **DWAYNE**.)*
>
> *(**VEE** addresses the crowd.)*

VEE. ...And now for our final presentation. Give it up for my pal Simon Branson.

> *(The crowd applauds politely as **SIMON** steps up. He clears his throat nervously and then begins.)*

SIMON. Hello, my name is Simon. So I – um – made a comic book. Not about a superhero or anything. Just sort of about...us... 'Cause I was thinking if the world might really end in a hundred years, we should start to look around and appreciate what we have, while we have it... And I guess the way we really heal the world is just to be kind. And take care of each other before it's too late...

> *(He presses play and his video piece is projected...)*

[MUSIC NO. 24 "IF I ONLY HAD ONE DAY (REPRISE)"]

> *(His project is a breathtaking comic book. The images unfold elegantly on screen to match his words.)*

IF I ONLY HAD ONE DAY
I'D WAKE UP WITH THE SUN.

GRATEFUL THAT THE DAY HAS JUST BEGUN.

AND THEN I'D HUG MY MOM A LITTLE LONGER

AND SAY:

"I'M SO GLAD WE HAVE TODAY."

AND LATER ON THAT DAY

WITH THE SUN NOW HIGH ABOVE

I WOULD TRY TO FIND THE PERSON THAT I LOVE.

I KNOW THAT SHE WOULD MAKE ALL OF MY WORRIES GO
AWAY...

ON THIS FINAL DAY.

OF COURSE, I'M SURE SHE HAS A MILLION THINGS TO DO.

OTHER FRIENDS AND FAM'LY SHE MUST REACH.

BUT WITH HER PHONE DESTROYED, MAYBE SHE'LL AVOID
ALL THAT

AND SIMPLY, HEAD TO THE BEACH.

AND THAT IS WHERE I'LL BE.

DRAWING ONE LAST SKETCH

THAT WOULD SHOW THOSE WHO MIGHT FIND IT,

WHAT I SEE:

MY MOM AND DAD, JIM, AND VEE

ALL THERE WITH ME

ON THIS SUDDENLY GREY, BUT PERFECT DAY.

> *(After he concludes, everyone applauds.* **VEE** *is quietly touched by his brave declaration... The crowd mills around, chatting and exploring the exhibits.)*

> *(***SIMON*** *finds* **VEE**, *who is standing with* **DWAYNE**.*)*

SIMON. Hey.

VEE. Hey.

SIMON. *(To* **DWAYNE**.*)* Can you give us a minute?

DWAYNE. Give you a minute?

SIMON. *(Firmly.)* That's right.

(DWAYNE looks at him, surprised. But SIMON has a new strength now, which DWAYNE feels... DWAYNE exits.)

VEE. Your presentation was really sweet.

SIMON. Thanks.

(A beat.)

VEE. Simon. About what you said up there... You know I think you're really nice, but...

SIMON. ...But.

VEE. ...Yeah. I really appreciate all you did for tonight and I hope we can still be friends.

SIMON. It's okay. I understand. I get it. It's fine. That was really stupid, saying all that.

VEE. No... It was brave.

(She gives him a quick kiss on the cheek and then exits.)

(SIMON stands for a moment, shattered.)

(CHARLOTTE, who has witnessed all of this from across the room, goes to him.)

CHARLOTTE. That was really incredible. I'm so proud of you, Simon.

SIMON. Thanks... Where's Jim?

CHARLOTTE. Honey, I'm sorry, but he didn't make it. He wasn't feeling well.

SIMON. He's not here?

CHARLOTTE. I'm sorry, no.

SIMON. Oh... That sucks. *That really sucks.*

(CHARLOTTE can see he's angry and hurt.)

CHARLOTTE. Simon, you know he gets these panic attacks...

SIMON. No, I understand. He has important things to do... It was just a stupid school thing, right?

CHARLOTTE. Come on, let me take you out to dinner.

SIMON. *(Snaps.)* I just need to be alone, okay?

(He goes quickly, before the tears come.)

[MUSIC NO. 24A "THE BEACH"]

Scene Fifteen
The Building

(Later that night.)

(CHARLOTTE sits on the stoop, deep in thought.)

(JIM enters. Heads toward her.)

JIM. Charlotte! Hey...

CHARLOTTE. It broke his heart.

JIM. What?

CHARLOTTE. Simon. It broke his heart when you weren't there tonight.

JIM. I'm so sorry, you know when I get these things there's nothing I can do –

CHARLOTTE. No, no. I understand. I'm not blaming you.

(Beat.)

(The moment has come.)

CHARLOTTE. He needs someone who's going to be there for him... So do I.

JIM. I understand.

CHARLOTTE. It's just where we are right now.

JIM. I'd kind of like to talk to Simon...

CHARLOTTE. Sure. He's up on the roof I think.

(Beat.)

JIM. Thank you... For getting me out of my apartment. For getting me out of my life I guess.

[MUSIC NO. 24B "FIRST STEPS"]

CHARLOTTE. First steps are hard...

JIM. Yeah... But we did it.

CHARLOTTE. We did.

> (**JIM** *exits into the building.*)
>
> (**CHARLOTTE** *sits.*)

Scene Sixteen
The Roof

> *(Almost dawn.)*
>
> (**SIMON** *is alone, drawing one of his comic books.)*
>
> (**JIM** *enters.)*

JIM. Hey.

SIMON. Hey.

> *(Beat.)*

JIM. I'm sorry about tonight. I wanted to be there.

SIMON. Don't worry about it.

JIM. No, I should have been there... Listen, your mom and I talked... We think it's best if we don't see each other anymore. It's a tough time for you guys, I get that.

SIMON. And what about for you?

JIM. Oh, I'll be all right... I was thinking of getting out of town anyway. Get a fresh start somewhere else.

SIMON. Please don't go.

JIM. I think it's best.

SIMON. I'll miss you.

JIM. Me too... But you know if you ever need me, I'll be here... Like I was that day.

> (**SIMON** *looks at him.)*

SIMON. *That day...*

JIM. I made a choice... But now that I know you, it's easier to live with... Take care of yourself, Simon. And your mom.

(He starts to go. Stops.)

Thanks for being my sidekick.

(He goes.)

(**SIMON** *is shattered, the revelation too much for him.)*

[MUSIC NO. 24C "FINAL ISSUE"]

(**CHARLOTTE** *enters.)*

CHARLOTTE. Simon... Come inside, we have to talk.

SIMON. Jim's gone.

CHARLOTTE. I know, honey. I'm sorry.

SIMON. He cared about us... We could have been a family.

CHARLOTTE. *We are a family.* You and me. That's what we have... Not Jim. Not Dad... And we have to try to say goodbye. Both of us.

SIMON. I've been trying, Mom... I have. I know you need to know what happened that day... I've been trying to understand it for two years...

(He hands her the comic book he was drawing.)

(**CHARLOTTE** *realizes. This is Simon's way of grappling with the trauma.)*

[MUSIC NO. 24D "THE COMIC BOOK"]

(**CHARLOTTE** *flips through the pages. We see the emotion growing on her face.)*

So I draw these things. I try to make the hero win. But it just doesn't... Dad was holding my hand. Like he always did... We stepped into traffic... And something pulled me back so I was safe... But Dad wasn't.

(**CHARLOTTE** *finishes the comic. Shuts it.)*

CHARLOTTE. Oh Simon.

SIMON. You can keep it. That's my last comic book. It's all bullshit.

CHARLOTTE. No, it's not.

SIMON. Of course it is! Useless drawings that do nothing! They give you a bunch of lies and you start believing in them.

[MUSIC NO. 25 "SUPERMAN IS DEAD"]

But why ever care about anyone?! They always leave!

CHARLOTTE. Simon, no –

SIMON. *(Melting down.)* They leave and you end up fucked. Like Vee. And Jim. *And Dad*. And you never get to say goodbye! Dad always said things would work out – but they don't!

I BELIEVED IN EV'RYTHING
I BELIEVED IN ALL THE STORIES THAT HE TOLD TO ME
THE LIFE AFFIRMING BULLSHIT THAT HE SOLD TO ME
BUT NOW I SEE...

THAT NOTHING CAN PROTECT ME FROM THE DARKNESS
NO ONE'S HERE TO TAKE AWAY THE DREAD –
THE BAD GUYS WON THE BATTLE
THERE'S CHAOS IN THE STREETS
AND SUPERMAN IS DEAD –
SUPERMAN IS DEAD.

YOU WERE ALWAYS EV'RYTHING
A CALMING VOICE AT TIMES THAT I WAS PETRIFIED.
YOU KNEW JUST WHAT TO SAY
TO MAKE MY FEAR SUBSIDE.
BUT I GUESS YOU LIED...

'CAUSE NOW YOUR CAPE LIES TATTERED, TORN TO PIECES
THE VIRUS OF DESPAIR CAN ONLY SPREAD
WE NEVER SAW IT COMING, IT TOOK OUR BREATH AWAY

SUPERMAN IS DEAD –
SUPERMAN IS...

HOW COULD IT HAPPEN, YOU ASK?
HOW COULD OUR GREATEST FEARS COME TO PASS?
AN ORDINARY DAY BECOMES A NIGHTMARE.
I THOUGHT YOU WERE UNSINKABLE
IMMUNE FROM THE UNTHINKABLE
BUT I WAS SO NAIVE AND UNAWARE
'CAUSE IT DIDN'T TAKE LEX LUTHOR, TO SEND YOU ON
    YOUR WAY
JUST A CAR THAT DIDN'T SEE YOU ON THAT BREEZY
    AUTUMN DAY
IF ONLY WE HAD MISSED THE BUS
IF ONLY I HAD HELD YOUR HAND
IF ONLY YOU WERE HERE RIGHT NOW, TO TELL ME IT
    WILL ALL BE OKAY...
BUT IT WON'T BE OKAY
NO IT WON'T BE OKAY

SO DIM THE LIGHTS AND PRAY FOR HE WHO'S FALLEN
RAISE THE FLAGS HALF-STAFF AS IT IS SAID
I TOOK IT ALL FOR GRANTED, AND NOW IT'S MUCH TOO
    LATE
SUPERMAN IS DEAD
SUPERMAN IS DEAD.
SUPERMAN IS –

CHARLOTTE. *Simon.*

[MUSIC NO. 23 "SUPERHERO"]

I WISH THAT THINGS WERE DIFF'RENT
I WISH YOUR DAD WERE HERE
I WISH THAT YOU AND I
WEREN'T FALLING FROM THE SKY
AND LIVING LIFE IN FEAR.

BUT IF I CAN'T THROW BOULDERS
OR CIRCLE 'ROUND THE EARTH

I CAN STILL HOLD ON TO YOU FOR ALL I'M WORTH

IF I CAN'T BE A SUPERHERO

I WILL STILL BE STRONG

I'LL TRY TO MAKE THINGS BETTER

I'LL WORK TO RIGHT WHAT'S WRONG

SO CLOSE THE COMIC BOOKS, MY BOY,

BUT KNOW THESE WORDS TO BE TRUE:

IF I CAN'T BE A SUPERHERO

I'LL STILL FIGHT FOR YOU

IT'S OKAY TO SAY YOU'RE ANGRY

IT'S OKAY TO JUST BE PISSED

BUT THIS HURT THAT WE CAN'T SEE –

IF YOU SET THE WHOLE MESS FREE

I SWEAR IT WON'T BE MISSED

'CAUSE YOU AND I CAN DO THIS

WE CAN MAKE IT ON OUR OWN

BUT I CAN'T TURN THIS THING AROUND IF I'M ALONE

'CAUSE I CAN'T BE A SUPERHERO

I'VE NO WINGS TO SOAR

OR SPIN THE PLANET BACK TO

THE WAY IT WAS BEFORE

AND WE BOTH KNOW IT'S NOT ENOUGH

TO JUST BE BRAVE AND GOOD

NO I CAN'T BE A SUPERHERO –

BUT HOW I WISH I COULD

SO SIMON, PLEASE BELIEVE IN SUPERHEROES

IN WARRIORS WHOSE POWERS ASTOUND

BUT SON OF MINE, REMEMBER SUPERHEROES

CAN BE FOLKS WHO KEEP THEIR FEET ON THE GROUND

WHO CAN'T JUST VANQUISH VILLAINS WITH A DAZZLING
    LASER-RAY

WHO'LL NEVER KNOW THE JOY IT IS TO FLY

WHOSE SUPERHUMAN STRENGTH IS JUST TO FACE
    ANOTHER DAY

IN A WORLD WHERE PEOPLE HURT

AND FATHERS DIE...

IF I COULD BE A SUPERHERO
I'D BRING HIM BACK FOR YOU
BUT THIS WORLD IS FOR MORTALS
IT'S LONELY, BUT IT'S TRUE
BUT EVEN SO, I PROMISE YOU
THAT SOMEDAY WE WILL BE FREE
I KNOW THAT I'M NO SUPERHERO
BUT IF YOU NEED A SUPERHERO
THAT'S WHAT I'LL TRY TO BE
BUT YOU'RE THE SUPERHERO TO ME.
TO ME.
TO ME...

> *(At the end of the song,* **SIMON** *suddenly hugs her deeply, totally breaking down. Breaking through.)*

> *(They cling together. With hope. With love. Mother and son.)*

> *(Superheroes.)*

> *(As the dawn breaks.)*

The End